IT'S A KIND OF LOVE

GERRY CULLEN

Copyright © 2024 GERRY CULLEN

All rights reserved

The characters and events portrayed in this book are fictitious. Any similarity to real persons, living or dead, is coincidental and not intended by the author.

No part of this book may be reproduced, or stored in a retrieval system, or transmitted in any form or by any means, electronic, mechanical, photocopying, recording, or otherwise, without express written permission of the publisher.

ISBN-13: 9798327433304
ISBN-10: 1477123456

Cover design by: Art Painter
Library of Congress Control Number: 2018675309
Printed in the United States of America

THIS BOOK IS DEDICATED TO MY MUM AND DAD

CONTENTS

Title Page
Copyright
Dedication
ALSO BY gERRY CULLEN
About The Author   298
Praise For Author   300
Books By This Author   304

ALSO BY GERRY CULLEN

BETWEEN WORLDS:

MY TRUE COMA STORY

SKY HIGH: COTE D'AZUR

ANGEL'S EYES:

CHRISTMAS ANGELS

THE VATICAN MONSIGNOR

– THE SAVIOUR'S COMING

GERRYCULLEN

IT'S A KIND OF LOVE

This Book is based on a true and original story.

The setting is LEEDS and other locations.

Although most of the story is real, some scenes and locations have been created for comedy/drama purposes.

I hope you thoroughly enjoy my story!

About The Author

GERRY CULLEN

My first book, BETWEEN WORLDS: MY TRUE COMA STORY, is a true adaptation of what happened to me, before and after, having major open heart surgery at Leeds General Infirmary in March 2018.

It is a very real and true account of the "gift" I received after being in an induced coma.

All of my books to date, SKY HIGH! COTE D'AZUR, ANGEL'S EYES/CHRISTMAS ANGELS, and THE VATICAN MONSIGNOR are adapted from my series of stories, written for television.

I had never written books or for television prior to being in a coma.

My very real and true story continues today!

FOLLOW MY STORY ON TWITTER - @GerryCullen15

IT'S A KIND OF LOVE

It's back to 1987 for this Singled Out themed comedy/drama series of stories set in Leeds.

This book is based on an original, and true story, up to the end of 1991.

What happens after that continues into 1992 with the ITV Telethon.
Everything is based on real people, real parties and real events.

The locations and venues of IT'S A KIND OF LOVE tell one man's story, and the challenges he faces, after joining a national Singles Organisation!

We commence in Leeds city centre, where various characters are introduced at Zodiac, and then again at Mirage.

Zodiac and Mirage are Social/Single Organisations which have been set up UK wide. Both are run privately, by the members.

This is a time when there were no mobile phones, laptops or the Internet! When we spoke of a tablet it was usually to take away pain, and not an electrical device connected to the Internet!

Everyone used ordinary house telephones, and call

boxes to get in touch, with each other.

We used A to Z map books to find addresses and locations.
Satellite for cars had not yet been invented!
Pop music and fashions were top of the list.

Gez moves in to an apartment on the outskirts of Leeds, and decides to join Zodiac.

IT'S A KIND OF LOVE tells his real story!

From joining to attending parties, and events ... to meeting lots of ladies ... getting sound advice ... to running his own event disco's on a grand scale!

This all eventually leads to events for ITV TELETHON 1990 and 1992, and a main arena event in the grounds of HAREWOOD HOUSE on the outskirts of Leeds.

But Gez is hiding something ...

Who is he, and where did he come from?

Why is he hiding a secret?

New adventures lie before him, but will he find love or won't he?

Why does he have so many female admirers at

Zodiac?

Will all eventually be revealed?

LEADING MALE CHARACTERS

MIKE – Mike is five foot ten, in his mid forties, has brown hair, and green eyes, stocky build … a man about town, and a bit of a Jack the lad! Mike is basically a man's man! He knows what he wants and how to get it! Mike is next to the main man at Zodiac in Leeds, and he runs the Bar Nights at Tapas. Well respected by all Zodiac members, Mike tells it how it is! Has a certain way with the ladies! Good friend of Ernest and Gez.

ERNEST- Ernest is five foot ten, in his sixties, has long white hair, brown eyes, clean shaven, and very much a bit of a charmer!

He's got a talent for putting his foot in it, big time … but he doesn't care!

He certainly knows how to get a ladies attention.
King of the one liners! Ernest has got the gift of the gab! Great mates with Mike and Gez!

Ernest, is a one man show, on his own!

Brilliant laugh lines throughout!

His wit and humour light up many stories! A decorated World War 2 fighter pilot, in real life!

This character was based on him!

GEZ – Mystery man … no one knows who he really is!

Gez is 6ft tall, and in his mid thirties, has brown hair, and blue eyes, attractive.

Seems to be hiding a secret, but nobody can get close

enough to find out what it is!

Mike and Ernest, work in contrast and guide Gez all the way to eventual success, even though they take the mickey out of him!

Gez seems to have lots of admirers at Zodiac.

DAVID – enigmatic Manager of Zodiac, Leeds … affectionately known as Mr Leeds!

David is in his late 40s, has dark hair, and is a cool character … keeps it all together, and is a stickler for getting everything right!

If anyone puts a foot wrong @ Zodiac, David is the man to sort it out!

LEADING FEMALE CHARACTERS

JANE - Jane is slim, very attractive, and has short dark hair, well groomed and stylish, wears the fashions of the day. She knows how to get a man's attention, and how to make them pay attention to her! Life and soul of the party!
LUCY - Lucy has shoulder length blonde hair, very slim and very attractive too.
Best friend and confidant to Jane!
Both are style icons from York!
Likes to take charge of situations and manipulate events. Lots of style and panache from both ladies!

CARLA - Carla is five foot seven, has long brown hair, and very pretty. She is in her early thirties!
Looking for love or maybe just anyone who has a pulse!
In pursuit of Gez from first introduction!
Will she get her man?

SALLY - Sally is five foot six, has blonde curly hair, has green eyes, in her early thirties and pretty!

She is in Carla's shadow, and both seem to be on the hunt for a man in their lives! But will she find love or get dumped at the first hurdle?

KRIS – Kris is five foot eight, has short brown bobbed

hair, brown eyes and attractive! Has a mischievous glint in her eye, and possesses a wicked sense of humour! Will her charms and personality sway Gez to fall for her?

WHAT TV PRODUCTION COMPANIES ARE SAYING ABOUT IT'S A KIND OF LOVE

Thank you for sending IT'S A KIND OF LOVE for us to review. What can I say? It was a thoroughly enjoyable ride, all the way! I loved reading about Zodiac, and the Singles club scene.
I do think there is something very interesting in watching something like that in contrast to today's more impersonal online dating.
It's seems to be so personal, and on another level!
Your characters and situations were classic and timeless. We got to know them all personally.
Your main characters, Mike and Ernest, worked in contrast and guided Gez all the way to eventual success, even though they took the mickey out of him!
The Female leads, Jane, Lucy, Carla and Sally were also very much part of the situation surrounding Gez.
He certainly has lots of admirers!
Ernest, was a one man show, on his own!
Brilliant laugh lines throughout!

His wit and humour lit up many stories, and then to find out that he really was a decorated World War 2 fighter pilot, in real life, was unreal!

I really liked the fact that we could tell there was a secret lurking under the surface of Gez. I thought that worked nicely with the storyline.

It's only at the end of your book, when Gez's story takes another turn.

Bearing that in mind, it worked very well with the title and the cover design of your book.

That alone threw me completely off the scent, but I now realise that it works very well with your cliff hanger ending, and that it is only in your follow up book when the aura surrounding Gez will be fully revealed!

Having said that, I think it will take the readers by surprise!

Thank you for submitting your series for review, and I wish you well and every success with it!

- LIVERPOOL PRODUCTION COMPANY

IT'S A KIND OF LOVE

NEW BEGINNINGS 6

RING OUT THE OLD …
RING IN THE NEW 18

SHIPS THAT PASS IN
THE NIGHT 30

NO MAN IS AN ISLAND! 37

THE LIFE AND SOUL
OF THE PARTY 51

DECORATING THE
LOO PARTY 58

ZODIAC CHRISTMAS
DINNER DANCE 67

ERNEST'S SURPRISE
PARTY 72

NEW YEAR'S EVE BASH 81

*CHRISTMAS IN JULY/
SUMMER BAR BQ 92*

A NEW FOUND

CONFIDENCE 109

*CLOSE ENCOUNTERS OF ...
THE FEMALE KIND! 133*

*ZODIAC REVIEW- THE EVENT:
A CELEBRATION DISCO 147*

*AS ONE DOOR CLOSES
... CALLING ELVIS 150*

*A SQUARE PEG IN A
ROUND HOLE/CHRISTMAS
EVENT 158*

*YOU CAN GET IT IF YOU
REALLY WANT IT! 164*

*A WORD IN YOUR
SHELL LIKE! 171*

*I'LL GO WHERE THE
MUSIC TAKES ME! 177*

NEW BEGINNINGS

When Gez sets up home at a studio flat in Headingley, he decides to change his life forever, by joining a Singles Club in Leeds. However, he is totally unaware of the adventures that lie before him, or the challenges that lie ahead!
Suddenly, the phone rings in the furnished flat. Gez picks up the receiver …
"Hello" answers Gez
"Just checking to see if you are settling in?" asks a voice
"Yes, I'm more than comfortable, thank you" replies Gez
"Well, if there's anything we can do, remember, we are only a phone call away" advises the voice
"Yes, I'll remember, thanks, again" replies Gez

The call ends. Gez picks up the Evening Post newspaper and begins to read it. After reading all about the current news, he sees an advertisement in the Personal Column for Zodiac, in the centre of Leeds.
Gez decides to take the plunge and makes the call to Zodiac.

The phone begins to ring, and then it is answered by a well mannered man.

"Hello, my name is David … how can I help you?" asks the voice

"Oh, I'm thinking of joining Zodiac, David" advises Gez

"It's my absolute joy, and pleasure in life, to welcome you" quips David

"Hi, my name is Gez"
"Well, you've come to the right place, Gez" replies David

"It costs £80 a year to join, but you can pay that over three months … are you still interested, Gez?" asks David
"Oh, definitely, David" replies Gez

"We charge that amount, basically to deter the lower end of the market from joining" explains David
"But, as I said, you can pay it in three monthly instalments, Gez" replies David
"Well, David, I am really interested" advises Gez
"OK, if you can post three signed cheques … two for £26 each, dated at monthly intervals and one for £28 dated today … then we're in business" replies David
"Yes, I'll get my payments off to you today" advises Gez
"OK, this is the address, Gez" advises David

"When we receive your cheques we'll set the wheel in motion" explains David

"We'll send out by post, your red membership card and the Zodiac magazine on receipt" replies David
"Zodiac is a nationwide organistion" advises David

"Sounds exactly what I'm looking for" replies Gez
"Believe me, you've made the right decision Gez … your social life will soar" explains David
"You'll also have complete anonymity here, members are only known by their first names" advises David
"Surnames and addresses are never disclosed" explains David

"Wow, it all sounds fantastic, David … just what I'm looking for" replies Gez

"OK, you should receive all the information by post, in a couple of days" advises David
"I'll get it off to you tonight"
repliess David
"Thank you, David" responds
Gez
"It's my absolute pleasure" quips David
"The next Bar Night is on Tuesday evening at Tapas in Lower Briggate" explains David
"Do you know where it is?" adds David
"Don't worry I'll find it" adds Gez
"Excellent, I'm looking forward to going there, already" replies Gez
"Yes, go to the Bar night on Tuesday" advises David
"Mike will meet and greet you there … he will also brief you about everything else" explains David
"Thanks, David, I can't wait" replies Gez

A couple of days pass, and the postman puts a large

envelope through Gez's letter box.
Gez reads all the information and the Zodiac monthly magazine, cover to cover. It's packed with tips and events which are taking place all over the UK.
Eventually, Tuesday evening arrives. Gez makes his way into Leeds and parks his car in Sovereign Street, which is close to Lower Briggate.
It's October 1987, just a few days before Halloween!

Gez walks up Lower Briggate and finds Tapas which is situated underneath an iron railway bridge, below the busy main thoroughfare.
Zodiac is a Singles Organisation with branches all over the UK.
It's prime directive is to bring together single people, from all walks of life, and provide social activities in a friendly atmosphere.
It is run, exclusively, by the members.
Tapas Bar has plush surroundings and a seating and standing area. There is a dance area to the left and it has a regular DJ on Bar nights!

Tuesday evening, 8pm … close to the bar area.

Gez enters the ambient surroundings where he is met by Mike, who is in his forties, and a bit of a Jack the lad.
"Hi … I'm Mike" greets a voice (Both shake hands)
"Hello Mike … I'm Gez" replies
Gez (Smiling)
"Welcome to Tapas … and

Zodiac" enthuses Mike
"Is it your first night, Gez?" asks Mike
"Yes, afraid so … can you show me the ropes, Mike?" replies Gez

"Well, best thing to do is check out our events board, over there, and see what takes your fancy" advises Mike (Points over to the wall next to the Bar)
"Grab yourself a beer, then come back here, I'll introduce you to one or two members" explains Mike
"OK, I'll take a look … thanks Mike" replies Gez (Smiling)

Gez is away for a few minutes, making note of a party at the weekend. Gez returns to Mike, where several other members are now congregating.

"Seen anything?" asks Mike
"There's a Halloween party in Knaresborough at the weekend" replies Gez
"I'll get a ticket for that … are you going Mike?" asks Gez
"Maybe … let me introduce you to Ernest, now he will be definitely going" answers Mike
"Everyone knows Ernest" explains Mike (Laughing)

"He's got a talent for putting his foot in it … but he doesn't care" advises Mike

Ernest is in his early sixties, has long white hair, and a charmer.

"Well, I told the ladies they could have my body for nothing last time ... and it worked" advises Ernest
Everyone is laughing at
Ernest's remarks!
"Smooth operator" replies
Mike (Laughing)
"See what I mean?" asks Mike
(Laughing)
"It all sounds a lot of fun" replies Gez (Now also Laughing)

Gez begins to introduce himself to several members.

"I'm Gez, by the way … first night for me"

advises Gez (Smiles)

"Pleased to meet you Gez" answers Ernest

Gez is in his mid thirties, tall, slim and attractive.

"Gez, buy a ticket for the Halloween party in Knaresborough for this Saturday, and go and enjoy yourself" recommends Ernest (Laughing)
"Yes, I will, Ernest" replies Gez

"Let your hair down, just like me" replies Ernest (Everyone Laughing)

"Will you be there, Ernest?" asks Gez
"Yes, I'll be there … and after you've been to a few events you'll become popular at Bar nights" explains Ernest
"Just like me" adds Ernest
(Laughing)
Everyone laughs at Ernest's
comical remarks.
"Ernest, your a breath of fresh air" advises Gez

"Oh please … please don't encourage him" laughs Mike

Saturday, 31st October, Halloween Party, Knaresborough …
Gez makes the journey from Leeds by car.
He eventually finds the address with his new A to Z map book.

He parks his car close to the house, where the party is taking place.

A string of balloons tied on a bush indicate it's the right house.

Gez knocks on the door of the party venue.

Lots of members are in fancy dress.

"Hi … thanks for coming to my party … I'm Anita" greets a voice (Big Smile)

"Oh Hi … I'm Gez" (Smiling)

Gez is dressed in a white shirt with black tie and black trousers.

"Are you from over here, honey?" asks Anita (Smiling)

"Oh, I'm from near Leeds, this is my first Zodiac party" advises Gez

"OK, well mingle honey, lots of ladies for you tonight" explains Anita

"Bottles and plates over there, love" points Anita (Big Smile)

"Thanks, Anita … I will" answers Gez (Smiling)

The party starts to get into full swing with lots of pop music blaring out.

Gez decides to mingle and meets two ladies straight away.

"Hi, were Miranda and Emily" advises a voice

Miranda is a tall red head with a beaming smile. Emily is a busty blonde.

"Oh, Hi … I'm Gez" (Smiles)

"Is it your first night, love?" asks Miranda (Smiling)
"Yes" replies Gez (Smiling)
"You?" asks Gez

"Oh, were veterans … this is our third party, honey" replies Emily (Smiling)

The music is suddenly turned up.

Several Halloween hits are now being played.

"Come and join us both on the floor" advises Miranda (Smiles)
Gez has no choice as he is virtually dragged onto the dance floor by Emily …
"OK, girls … don't mind if I do" replies Gez (Smiling)
"You really have no choice in the matter" laughs Emily
"It's a fun night, tonight" advises Gez (Smiles)
"Oh, we like fun, love" answers Emily (Beaming)

"So, you been married then?" asks Miranda

"Oh no … not me … had a few false alarms, you know" replies Gez (Smiling)

"False alarms?" asks Emily (Looks puzzled)
"Oh, we know honey, we know" replies Miranda (Smiling)
"Have you both been married before?" asks Gez
"Oh yea … but you won't hold that against us, will you?" replies Emily

"No, of course not" replies Gez

Miranda pulls Gez towards her and starts to hold him close.

"Is that a gun you have in your pocket, or are you just pleased to see me?" asks Miranda (Smiling)
"Cheeky" replies Gez (Laughing)

"Wow … you girls are a bit forward"
replies Gez (Laughing)

"No use beating about the bush, love"
replies Emily (Laughs)

"I like your style" answers a voice (Laughing)
"Well, if it isn't Ernest" replies Gez

"Are you having a good time, Gez?" asks Ernest (Laughing)

"Oh, in my element … very pretty girls tonight" answers Gez (Smiling)

"Careful … they'll all be after you" replies Ernest (Laughing)
"OK, girls … I'm going to take a breather" advises Gez
"Hurry back, honey" reply both girls
(Big smiles)
Gez leaves the dance area with Ernest.

"Come on lad, you look as though you could do with a drink?" advises Ernest

"What have you brought with you?" asks Ernest
"A few cans of non alcoholic

beer" replies Gez

"Oh, that's not for me" replies
Ernest (Laughing)

"Well, I am driving" replies Gez

Gez decides to leave the bar area and bumps straight into Nick.

"Hi, I'm Nick from York ... I sort of look after the York Bar Night ... hope you'll join us sometime" advises Nick

"Hi, Nick ... I'm Gez ... this is my first party ... I'm from Leeds" replies Gez

"Oh, I see you've settled in already. I saw you dancing with Miranda and Emily" advises Nick (Winking)

"You know them?" asks Gez

"Yea, I know them" replies Nick (Laughing)

"Well, you know ... they have such terrific taste" explains Nick (Laughs)

Both Gez, Nick and Ernest are in stitches with laughter.

The DJ suddenly plays ... Simply the Best by Tina Turner ...

Suddenly two more lovely ladies arrive on the scene.

"Hi ... we're Jane and Lucy, from York" advises a voice

"I was just about to introduce you both" replies Nick (Laughing)

"This is Gez ...he's from Leeds" advises

Nick (Smiling)

"They'll take you under their wing ... look after him, love" advises Nick (Winks)

"Oh, we will ... we will darling" answers Jane (Big smile)

Jane is slim, very attractive, and has short dark hair, well groomed and stylish, wearing the fashions of the day. Lucy has shoulder length blonde hair, very slim and very attractive too.

"Come on, Gez this is Zodiac's anthem, lets go on the floor, darling" advises Jane

Everyone piles on to the dance floor, including Ernest.

"Care to dance with us ... are you up for it and can you handle us both?" asks Lucy (Big smile)

"Is that a trick question?" asks Gez (Laughing)

"We don't do trick or treat, honey ... but you can trick and treat us if you want to" replies Jane (Smiling)

"Well, I suppose it is Halloween" replies
Gez (Laughing)

"Everyone's in need of a good scare"
advises Lucy

"Your in good company" advises Jane

"Oh, I know ... your both charming, very attractive ladies, and very elegant too" replies Gez

"Flattery will get you everywhere, young man" replies Jane (Smiling)

"You've also obviously got great taste" replies Gez

"We're from York, love … and we know who, and what we like" replies Lucy "You'll never forget us, will you?" asks Jane (Big Smile)

"Your so right, Jane … I won't" replies Gez (Smiling)

"You'll be walking on air, tonight" advises Lucy (Laughing)

"Will you come to see us in York, Gez?" asks Jane

"Well, you never know, Jane" replies Gez

"Our Bar night is on Thursday's" advises Jane

"We'll both be at Tapas, on Tuesday" advises Lucy (Smiling)

"Oh, I'll look forward to seeing you both there, then" replies Gez

"Count on it, darling" advises Jane (Big Smile)

At the next Bar night, Gez arrives at Tapas and is quizzed by Mike and Ernest about his first party in Knaresborough.

"Hi Gez … how did you get on at the party in Knaresborough?" asks Mike

"Oh, I met quite a few ladies that night" replies Gez

"So, the sound advice worked?" asks Mike (Laughing)

"Oh, yes, I was very impressed" replies Gez

"That's it … be confident, talk to people … make yourself known" replies Mike

"Oh, I did … and they did their bit too" replies Gez

(Laughing)
Ernest walks in and asks Gez for an update about the party ...
"Yea, but did you pull?" asks Ernest (Smiling)
"Well, Ernest ... let me get my feet under the table first" replies Gez (Laughing)
 "Not everyone's a Casanova, like you" replies Mike (Laughing)
"Well, when you've got it ... flaunt it" replies Ernest (All Laughing)
 "How does he do it?" asks Gez (Smiling)
"How does he get away with it" replies Gez (Laughing)

"Oh, they know him ... and I guess they love him for it" replies Mike (Laughing)

"Ernest's never short of a lady, on his arm" explains Mike (Laughing)
"Good luck to you, Ernest" replies Gez (Laughing)

The door to Tapas opens, Jane and Lucy enter the ambient surroundings.

"Well, hello boys ... lovely to see you all again" advises Jane (Big Smile)

"Hello, to you too, love" replies Mike (Smiling)
"You seemed to enjoy yourself on Saturday, Gez?" asks Jane (Beaming)
"Well, you spoilt me with your company" replies Gez (Smiling)
"Oh, we like to please, love" advises Lucy

"Hello, nice to see you girls, again" advises Ernest (Smiling)

"Oh, it's our pleasure, honey" replies Jane
"No, the pleasures all mine" insists Ernest (Laughing)
The DJ starts to play pulsating 80s pop music …
"May I have the pleasure?" asks Gez (Smiling)
"… of asking you for a dance?" replies Gez

"Your very polite, darling, OK lead on" replies Jane (Big Smile)

The music becomes quite intense, and the floor begins to fill up …

"Thanks for helping out with Ernest" advises Gez

"Oh, he can be overpowering" replies Lucy

"Think nothing of it, honey … always glad to help" responds Jane
"Are you both going to any Christmas parties?" asks Gez

"Oh, yes … and you must come too … we'll be puckering up" advises Jane

"Puckering up?" asks Gez (Looks puzzled)
"You know … kissy … kissy" replies Jane (Smiling)

"Oh, I'll definitely be there then" answers Gez (Smiling)

Jane and Lucy both laugh.
"There's one on Saturday, mid December, fancy going to that?" asks Jane
"Oh, where is it taking place?" asks Gez
"Another one in Knaresborough"
advises Lucy
"Don't they have parties in Leeds?" asks Gez
"Yes, naturally, but this is a Christmas disco, honey" advises Jane

"It's being held in the Parish Church Hall overlooking the River Nidd" explains Lucy
"OK, count me in … as long as you two are going" advises Gez
"We are … we'll be your Christmas fairies" replies Lucy
"Wow" laughs Gez
"Can't wait for that one" replies Gez

The Tapas DJ now plays Simply the Best by Tina Turner. All the dance floor starts to fill up.
"Oh, you must stay on for this … it's the Zodiac anthem" advises Jane
"Do I have a choice?" asks Gez
"Not really"
answers Jane
"OK, I will" replies
Gez
"Well, are we your favourite girls, Gez?"
asks Jane (Big Smile)
"Undoubtedly … your my only girls"

laughs Gez
"Have you been married,
honey?" asks Jane
"No … have you?" asks Gez
(Smiles)
"Oh, yea … afraid so" explains Jane (Big Smile)

"Well, I wont hold it against you" laughs Gez

"Oh, I was counting on you holding something against me" replies Jane (Cheeky)

"Well, you never know your luck, Jane" replies Gez (Looks embarrassed)

"You never know your luck" laughs Gez
"Don't get your knickers in a twist"
adds Jane (Laughing)
"I won't if you won't, love" replies
Gez
"You can count on it, honey" laughs Jane

RING OUT THE OLD …
RING IN THE NEW

Another Tuesday evening at Tapas. Ernest is in the party mood, and clearly up for anything … and everything!
"It's a war zone out there"
laughs Ernest
"What do you mean?" asks
Gez (Looks puzzled)
"Oh, I'm having to fight them off"replies Ernest (Laughing)
"There's just not enough of me to go round" laughs Ernest
"Are you popular or what?" asks Mike (Laughing)
"Well, there's life in the old dog yet" replies Ernest (All Laughing)
"You said it" laughs Mike (More Laughing)
"I don't know how he does it" asks Gez

"Viagra mate … me old pal, Viagra" answers Ernest (Everyone Laughing)

"Rock hard Gezza … rock hard" laughs Ernest
"OK … we get the picture, Ernest"
laughs Mike
"He's got the invisible touch alright" replies Gez
"We're all going to the Christmas party in

Knaresborough on Saturday … are you up for it Gez?" asks Mike (pointing to the Events board)
"Oh, yea … can't disappoint Jane and Lucy" replies Gez
"Oh, they can charm the pants off anyone" advises Mike
"Well, they can have the pants off me anytime" answers Ernest (All Laughing)
"What's he on?" asks Gez (Laughing)
"Whatever it is, it's working" laughs Mike

"Well, we all know the answer to that don't we?" asks Gez (Laughing)
Saturday arrives, and the Christmas Party in Knaresborough is billed as the event of the year. Zodiac, Harrogate are the instigators of the evening …
Mike, Ernest and Gez arrive at the Parish Church venue and are met by the lady in charge of the party.
"Hi, I'm Diana … thanks for coming to my do" advises Diana

Diana is a full bodied lady, dressed up to the nines in her red dress …

"Hi, I'm Gez … it's a nice venue, Diana" replies Gez
"Oh, we've used it a few times … by the way I'm the Harrogate organiser on behalf of Zodiac" advises Diana (Big Smile)
"It's going to be a Christmas party with a bang" explains Diana (Smiling)
"Oh?" asks Gez

"Fireworks at Midnight, love" replies Diana (Big Smile)

"Oh, I thought you were talking about Ernest" answers Mike (Laughing)

"Hi Mike … I didn't know you were coming?" replies Diana (Big Smile)

"Oh, I thought I'd come along and show my face" laughs Mike

"And … very wise too" replies Diana (Laughing)

"We're having a buffet … did you remember to bring your bottle, and something to eat for the table?" asks Diana (Points to Kitchen area)

"Of course we did … they are already there" advises Ernest (Smiling)

"OK, thanks" replies Diana

The disco starts up and various Christmas hits are playing …

"Come on … everyone on the dance floor" asks Mike (Pointing)

"Yea, look where Ernest's got his hands" advises Gez (Laughing)

"Not down his trousers, I hope?" replies Mike (All Laughing)

"No … on someone's backside" replies Gez (More Laughing)

"… and the party has only just begun" laughs Mike

"You've got to hand it to him … Ernest is a fast worker" replies Mike (Laughing)

More Christmas favourites are now being played by the DJ …
"They are playing my song" shouts Ernest (Laughing)
"Is he OK, Mike?" asks Gez (Looks concerned)
"Keep an eye on him, mate" advises Mike

Mike leaves the floor and heads towards the bar area.

Gez is left on his own, but not for long …
"Hi Gez, I'm Paula … I've been sent over by Mike, to look after you" says a voice
"Oh really … well Mike always did have good taste" replies Gez (Laughing)
Paula is a slim brunette with blue eyes, and tantalising statistics.
"Come on Paula … looks like you've pulled" advises Gez (Laughing)
"And what of Mike?" asks Paula
"Oh, he's in deep conversation with your friend" advises Gez

"Oh, Sacha, my friend … Mike told me to keep you company" replies Paula

"Well, that's what friends are for, love" explains Gez (Laughing)
"You are so right, honey"
replies Paula
"I like your outfit"

responds Gez

Paula is dressed in an all red outfit and decorated with tinsel ...

"I'm glad you approve" advises Paula

"It fits in all the right places, love" adds Gez (Smiling)

"I'm so glad you noticed, love" replies Paula (Beaming)

"We have to impress our would be admirers don't we?" adds Paula

"Would be?" asks Gez

"Well ... you would ... wouldn't you?" laughs Paula

"Would what?" replies Gez (Looking embarrassed)

"Want to be with me" explains Paula

"Oh, yea ... now I get it" answers Gez (Laughing)

"Well, you will ... if you play your cards right" advises Paula

"Oh ... I always watch Brucie" replies Gez

"Well, you might get a Brucie bonus tonight, love" laughs Paula

"Is this a joke ... it's a wind up right?" asks Gez (Laughing)

"No, straight up ... it's not a wind up ... I fancy you" explains Paula

"Hello ... are you talking to me?" asks Gez (Looks embarrassed)

"It must be a dream" laughs Gez

"It's no dream, honey … this is the real thing" replies Paula

"Wow" replies Gez

The DJ begins to play several more Christmas hits …

"Fancy a smooch, Gez?" asks Paula

"Oh … OK, Paula" replies Gez

Gez and Paula hit the dance floor …

"Wow … you dance real close" advises Gez

"No use not being close, is it?" asks Paula

"Your so charming … your not like the others" advises Paula

"Oh, is that what you think, Paula?" replies Gez

"Well, remember the one about wolves in sheep's clothing?" asks Gez

"Your not are you?" asks Paula

"No, I'm not" replies Gez

"Lucky you" explains Gez

The DJ changes the party mood and begins to play … SIMPLY THE BEST by TINA TURNER …

Everyone in the room piles on to the makeshift dance floor.

Gez bumps into Mike …

"Thanks, Mike" advises Gez

"Thanks for what?" asks Mike

"Oh, Paula" replies Gez

"Oh, she's a nice girl ... and your nice too ... I thought you'd appreciate each others company" advises Mike (Laughing)

"You'll only find quality here, Gez ... sheer quality" explains Mike (Laughing)

Gez and Paula continue to dance the night away, together.

"It's been another great night in Knaresborough" advises Gez

"Well, Paula ... it's the end of the night" explains Gez

"Do you want to come back to mine, for coffee, love?" asks Paula

"Let me think about it" advises Gez

After a wonderful Christmas, 1987 is set to end with a bang, at a New Year's Eve Party in Huddersfield and at Tapas in Leeds.

Tuesday Evening, Tapas, Lower Briggate, Leeds ... a few days before New Year.

"Have you got your ticket for the New Year's Eve bash, Mike?" asks Gez (Smiles)

"Oh, yea ... make sure you get yours" replies Mike

"Oh, I've just got mine tonight"

replies Gez

"Is it fancy dress?" asks Gez

"No … I think it's optional … casual, you know" advises Mike

"Good, that'll suit me just fine" replies Gez

"Me, too" replies Mike

A few days later, it's the biggest and most expensive night of the year ... New Year's Eve.
Gez arrives at the party, somewhere in Huddersfield ...

"Hi ... Welcome ... I'm Phil ... you found us alright?" asks Phil

"Yea, the A to Z worked just fine ... by the way, I'm Gez from Leeds" advises Gez

"Hi Gez" replies Phil (Both shake hands)
"OK ... make yourself at home ... food and drink in the kitchen please ... someone will help you" advises Phil (Pointing to the Kitchen)
"We're in for a great night ... bubbly at Midnight ... then we'll ring out the old and ring in the new to Big Ben's chimes" explains Phil
"Then, there's the haggis" advises Phil (Laughing)

"Haggis?" asks Gez (Looks stunned)
"Have you tried haggis before, Gez?" asks Phil
"No, not really, mate" replies Gez (Laughing)
"Oh yea, it's all part of the evening" explains Phil

Gez begins to mingle with all the other Zodiac members ...

"Hi, I'm Gez from Leeds"
"Oh, hi ... I'm Tony ... I'm from Leeds too" says a voice

"Snap ... well I'm from near Leeds, actually" replies Gez

"Is it your first night, Tony?" asks Gez

"Yes, it is" advises Tony (Looks serious)

"Have you been here before?" asks Tony

"Oh, yea ... a veteran now ... I've been a few times" explains Gez (Laughing)

"There are so many ladies here tonight, you'll be spoilt for choice" advises Gez

"That's what I'm looking for" laughs Tony
The music starts to play ... Tony and Gez decide to try their luck ...
"Not heard this one for a while" advises Tony
"Fancy a dance, love?" asks Gez

"Oh, that would be nice"
replies the voice

"Hi, I'm Gez ... this is Tony"
says Gez
"Hi, I'm Tessa and that's Sharon" replies Tessa

Both girls are stylish and dressed as Sixties dancers ...

"Are you both from Huddersfield?"
asks Tony
"We are ... and you?" asks Tessa

"Oh, we're both from Leeds" replies Gez

"Fancy having your photos taken with us in

IT'S A KIND OF LOVE

the beer tent?" asks Tony

"Well OK … but we've only just met" replies Sharon
"Oh … we're practically married now" adds Tessa (Laughing)
"You've got to be joking, right?" asks Tony (Looks puzzled)
"Oh, they are Tony … take it in your stride, it's all part of the fun" explains Gez
"Oh … now I get it" laughs Tony
"OK, you two sit on those chairs and then lets have the ladies on your laps" asks Bob, who is taking the photos
"Well, yea … if you insist" replies Tessa (Big Smile)

Flash … picture taken … one for the album

"Now … let's make it interesting with a kiss" asks Bob

"Yea, but I don't fancy you" replies Tony (Laughing)

"Not me" laughs Bob
"OK … one … two … three … go for it" replies Bob
Flash … another picture … number two for the album
"I'm in Heaven" advises Tony (Laughing)
"Me too, Tony" replies Gez (Laughing)
"Time to dance now, boys"

advises Sharon
"Let's go for it" replies Tony
The DJ is now blasting out various rock standards …

"Did you like our little gift to you on New Year's Eve?" asks Tessa (Big Smile)

"It was superb" replies Gez
"You've made our night, love" replies Tony (Smiling)

The New Year's Eve party is now in full swing. Lots more members arrive at the party venue.
Enter Jane and Lucy from York … both are dressed as fairies … in very short skirts …
"Wow … I must've died and gone to Heaven" advises Tony
"I'm so happy" replies Gez (Laughing)
"We told you we'd be here Gez … who's your friend?" asks Jane (Winks)
"Oh, this is Tony … first night tonight, love" replies Gez (Smiling)
"What a night to join, Tony"
advises Jane
"Hi, I'm Jane and this is
Lucy" explains Jane
"OK, you boys … on the dance floor now" orders Jane

"No ifs or buts … you must obey your fairies" advises Lucy (Big Smile)

A lot of disco music is now being played and it has a strong beat.
Ernest arrives at the New
Year's bash …

"I can see your knickers"
laughs Ernest
"Oh, your meant to … it's part of the outfit"
replies Lucy (Laughing)
"You two are lucky boys tonight" advises Ernest

"Are we?" asks Gez (Looks puzzled)

"What do you think?" asks Ernest

"You be a good boy tonight,
Ernest" advises Gez

"Oh ... I'm slightly inebriated"
answers Ernest

"He's sloshed" replies Jane
"He needs a kind nurse" replies Gez (Laughing)

"I'm sure he'll get what he's looking for"
advises Tony (Laughing)

"Oh, he usually does" explains Gez
"OK, you two ... how about paying us
some attention?" asks Lucy
"Now, let's get back to the dancing"
advises Jane
The time seems to pass quickly, and it's now just
a few minutes to Midnight. The DJ plays various
American anthems to get everyone in the mood.
"Gotcha, where I want you, at last" advises Gez
"Well, what are you going to do about
it?" asks Jane
"Wait till, Midnight" answers Gez
The DJ stops the music and tunes into Big
Ben's bongs at Midnight ... HAPPY NEW YEAR
... 1988 ...
"It's Midnight ... all gather round for
Auld Lang Syne" asks Phil
"Time for the Bubbly" advises Rachel
"Happy New Year" shouts Phil

There is lots of kissing, and hugging on the dance floor ...

"Aren't you glad you met me?" asks Jane
"Absolutely honey ... well I'm over the moon" replies Gez
"OK, don't forget my kiss" replies Jane
"Happy New Year Darling" advises Gez
"Tony ... have you done the rounds?" asks Gez (Laughing)
"Well, you have to ... haven't you?" replies Tony (Laughing)
"OK ... I'll come with you ... mustn't get left out" replies Gez
Suddenly, the atmosphere is broken with the arrival of Rick dressed in a Spaceman suit, minus helmet.
"Oh, no ... look who's just arrived" advises Mike
"Who?" asks Gez (Looks around)
"I dislike that man ... well so called man" replies Ernest

"I bet he dresses up in women's clothing too" advises Mike (Laughing)

"Yea, I bet he does" replies Ernest (Laughs)
"OK, steady on ... give him enough rope and he'll hang himself" advises Mike (Everyone laughs)
"He lives in fantasy land, that bloke" explains Ernest

"I take it, he's not very well liked at all?" asks Gez
"Oh … you got it in one, Gezza" replies Mike
"Very disliked" advises Ernest

"… and you know what Rick rhymes with?" adds Ernest

"You'll be surprised though … he's got his followers" advises Mike

"Yea … I can believe that" replies Gez
"He's a real motor mouth" adds Ernest

"Anyway, lets get back to the party … and the girls" advises Mike

"I'm with you on that" replies Ernest
(Laughs)
"What about you Gezza?"
asks Mike
"Oh, he's with me" replies
Jane
"Well, I'll leave you to it … good on you Gezza" replies Mike (Smiling)
Lucy, Jane, Tony and Gez take to
the dance floor …
"Well, it's 1988 now, this is our
time" advises Jane
"OK, Gezza … what do you think of
Zodiac now?" asks Jane
"Oh … it's the tops, Jane" replies Gez
"… and I met you and Lucy … that was

a bonus" advises Gez (Smiling)
The DJ starts to play several 80s hits …
"They are playing our song, Jane"
advises Gez
   "Come and make your fairy happy" replies Jane
"Your wish is my command" responds Gez
Ernest is now on the dance floor, and taking full advantage of everyone …
"Look at me go" shouts Ernest
"Your a good friend, Ernest … I like you" advises Gez

"Thanks, lad … stick by me … we'll have a fabulous year" laughs Ernest

Mike also enters the dance floor …
"Mike … you've helped me so much … maybe one day I will be able to thank you and Zodiac" advises Gez
"What about a party in the future?" asks Mike
"Well, you never know" replies Gez
The DJ plays more pop music, and adds a Swinging Sixties mix …
"See, I told you it would be never ending" advises Jane
"Hey … don't forget about us" advises Paula and Sacha
"Your all on our radar" insists Tony (Laughing)
"What a first night you've had, Tony" replies Gez

"Oh, it's been the best … simply the best" replies Tony

The DJ now plays the Zodiac anthem … SIMPLY THE BEST by TINA TURNER …

"Here we go again"

advises Gez

"How did they know?"

asks Tony

"Oh, you said the magic

words" replies Jane

"It's the Zodiac theme"

advises Mike

"It really is the best mate" advises Gez (All Laughing)

SHIPS THAT PASS IN THE NIGHT

We are now firmly set in 1988. Another timeless era, when a lot happened for Gez at Zodiac!
Tuesday Bar night, Tapas, Lower Briggate, Leeds city centre.

Mike, Gez and Ernest are all congregating near the Bar area with several old and new members.
"Hi … we're Sharon and Adam"
advise a couple (Both smiling)
"Hi, I'm Gez, lovely to meet you
both" replies Gez (Smiles)
"I don't think we've met before, have we?" asks Adam (Looks serious)
"No, I can't say that we have" replies Gez
"I don't recall seeing you both here before" explains Gez

"Oh, we've been members for a while now … we like it at Tapas" replies Sharon

"What about you?" asks Adam

"I've been a member for a few months now … and I can tell you that I'm thoroughly enjoying myself at Zodiac" replies Gez (Smiling)
"Have you met Sam?"
asks Sharon

"No, not yet" replies
Gez

Sam is a petite young lady with green eyes, and long dark hair, in her late thirties.

"Sam, this is Gez, from the same part of the woods as you" advises Adam

"Well hardly honey … I'm a cockney girl you see … here's Helen, she's from Yorkshire" replies Sam

"Hello, Helen … pleased to meet
you" replies Gez

"So polite" laughs Sam

"Well, hello there, love" replies Helen

Helen has short blonde bobbed hair, in her late forties, quite charming.

"I hear your both from my neck of the woods?" asks Gez

"Well, true … except Sam, is a long way from home" advises Helen (Smiles)

"An East Ender?" asks Gez (Smiling)

"Oh, yea … well and truly, mate" replies Sam

"I've lived up here a long time now though" explains Sam

"Ere … are you any good at Ballroom?"
asks Sam

"No, sorry love … two left
feet" replies Gez

 "No matter" replies Sam
(Smiling)

The DJ ramps up the music and everyone takes to the dance floor in Tapas …

"Shall we have a dance?" asks Sam (Pointing)
"Yea … let's get our dancing shoes on … your lucky tonight" replies Gez
"What about you, Helen?" asks Gez (Smiling)

"Come on Helen, that goes for you too" advises Sam (Looks bossy)
"Don't worry, I'm coming too, love" laughs Helen
"Bit of a bossy clogs, isn't she?" advises Gez
"Oh … she can be quite an handful" replies Helen
"Yea, I bet … in more ways than one" adds Gez
"Yea, but can you handle me?" asks Sam
Tapas main door opens. Enter Tony followed by Jane and Lucy.

Sam and Helen leave the floor, followed by Gez

"I see we've just arrived in time" advises Jane (Smiles)

"What do you mean?" asks Gez (Looks puzzled)
"In time for a dance … come on darling, the only way is up for you" laughs Jane
Gez looks a bit embarrassed!
Tony meanders over to Mike, who is standing near the bar …

"How's tricks, Mike?" asks Tony (Smiling)

"Oh, just fab mate" replies Mike (Laughing)

"Your looking a bit flash tonight, Tony" asks Mike

"Oh, first impressions mate … you don't look so bad yourself" quips Tony

"I see Jane and Lucy have arrived from York" advises Tony (Smiling)

"Yea, I think she's got her eye on Gez" replies Mike

"He looks a little embarrassed" replies Tony (Smiling)

"Looks like it … why don't we give him a hand" asks Mike

"You get Lucy on the dance floor" advises Mike

"You know I might just do that … what about you, Mike?" replies Tony

"Oh, there's a pretty blonde I've got my eye on over there" replies Mike

"Your very smooth, Mike" replies Tony

"Oh, that's me … a smooth operator to the end" laughs Mike

"Time to work your magic" advises Tony

The DJ starts to play various 80s hits …

Tony asks Lucy on to the dance floor, and she is only too happy to oblige.

"Hi Jane/Gez … can we join you?" asks Tony

"We?" asks Jane

"Lucy is with me" laughs Tony

"Well, your already on the floor" laughs Jane

Gez looks to be a million miles away, and is caught out by Jane …

"You look to be deep in thought, darling … was it something I said?" asks Jane

"Oh, no … you've done nothing wrong, Jane" replies Gez

"Well, are you gonna give it up?" asks Jane

"You never know your luck, Jane" replies Gez

"Your a bit of a dark horse, aren't you?" asks Jane (Looks puzzled)

"You two at it again?" asks Lucy (Smiling)

"Oh, it's just a bit of banter, that's all" replies Gez

Tony, Lucy and Jane retract to the Bar.

"Coming Gezza?" asks Tony (Points to Bar)

"Oh, sorry … I've got to leave … something unexpected has just popped up" replies Gez

"Where are you going, darling?" asks Jane

"Sorry, I have to go" replies Gez (Waving)

The following Tuesday, at Tapas, a lot of the "talk" is about little Sharon and Adam.

Gez arrives and is greeted by Tony with the news.

"Have you heard the latest

gossip?" asks Tony
 "No, heard what, Tony?" asks
Gez (Looks puzzled)
"It turns out that Adam was still married, Zodiac have booted him out of the club, and cancelled his membership" replies Tony (Looks serious)
"Ships passing in the night" advises Mike

Everyone knows … if anything happens at Tapas, you can count on it going round and round here" explains Mike
"It's a bit of a scandal"
replies Tony
"Yes, I guess it is"
advises Mike
"What is?" asks Ernest
(Looks intrigued)
"Ships passing in the night"
replies Gez
"What are you on about,
lad?" asks Ernest
Mike decides to take Ernest to one side and bring him up to speed!
"Well, I never … who'd have thought it?" replies Ernest
"Poor Sharon … but no one is really bothered about her" advises Tony
"Well, yes it's true … Adam has been thrown out of the Club" explains Mike
"He was still a married man … and that's why" advises Mike

IT'S A KIND OF LOVE

"This is a Club for non married Single people only … David had no choice but to ask him to leave" explains Mike

"What's happened to Sharon?" asks Gez

"She's obviously very upset, and feels she's been used, but she's going to carry on regardless" replies Mike

"Sound advice" advises Ernest

It's true, Sharon did carry on for a while, but then suddenly disappeared into the sunset … never to be seen again!

"That's not going to happen to me" advises Gez

"What do you suggest, Mike?" asks Gez

"Well, it's OK to take out who you fancy here … just remember keep it under your hat … that way no one will know what's going on" replies Mike (Looks serious)

"Mike's right, lad" advises Ernest

"What's your take on it?" asks Gez (Looks concerned)

"Hear all … see all … and say nowt" replies Ernest (All Laughing)

"The very fact that all and sundry would talk behind your back is not appealing" advises Gez

"You have to look after yourself, and give them nothing to talk about" replies Mike (Looks serious)

"You have nothing to worry about" explains Mike
"Did she love him to death?" asks Tony
"No idea, mate" replies Mike
CASE CLOSED …

Tony looks at the Events Board, and is excited by what he reads …

"Do you fancy going to that Harrogate Party Night in Knaresborough?" asks Tony

"What another one" replies Mike (Laughs)
"It's in a Church Hall … sounds like fun" explains Tony
"So was the last one" replies Mike (Laughing)
"What's happening?" asks Gez

"It's a Bar BQ, this time, lad" advises Ernest

"OK, I'm up for it, Tony … lets go" advises Gez

Gez takes another call at his studio flat in Headingley …

"Hello" replies Gez (Looks anxious)
"We are just touching base" replies the caller
"Is everything under control" asks the caller
"Yes, I'm alright … and taking all precautions" replies Gez
"Remember, we are only at the end of the phone" advises the caller

"People have been asking about you" explains the caller
"I'm fine ... I just need time" replies Gez
The call ends.
The following Saturday arrives. Gez and Tony arrive at the venue in Knaresborough.
"Hi ... lovely to see you both again ... I'm Mason ... I meet and greet at the Harrogate Bar Night" says a tall refined gentleman
"Oh, Hi Mason ... I'm Gez, that's Tony ... we're both from Leeds" advises Gez
"Have you met Dee and Kate from Harrogate?" asks Mason
Dee is a classy blonde, Kate is a tall, slim brunette.
"No, Hi ... I'm Gez ... this is Tony" advises Gez
"Hi, I'm Dee, and this is Kate" replies Dee
"So, your both from Leeds?" asks Kate
"That's right, we both are" beams Tony
"It's a lovely summers evening, Kate ... shall we take a look at the Bar BQ?" asks Gez (Smiling)
"Oh yea ... the views are wonderful over the river" replies Kate (Big Smile)

The area around the River Nidd is very beautiful. There are many quintessential viewing points. It's breathtaking location is frequented by many

travellers and tourists during the day.
At night it is even more breathtaking.

"I'll, leave you Tony … to get to know Dee, OK?" asks Gez

"OK, see you soon, buddy" replies Tony
Kate and Gez join several other members looking out across the views from the Church Hall balcony … it's a warm summer's evening.
"So, have you been in Zodiac, long?" asks Kate
"Just a few months … and you?" replies Gez
"I've been a member for about six months" advises Kate
"What are you looking for?" asks Kate (Smiling)
Gez is gobsmacked by that question, then decides to answer it tactically!
"Oh, a good social life … and then who knows" advises Gez (Very cautious)
"What about you?" asks Gez

"Oh, just socialising … I've just seen husband number two off" explains Kate (Looks sad)

"Really?" replies Gez
BLA BLA BLA … Kate goes into raptures about her past, and it gets boring …
"I'm just going for another beer, love … do you want a refill?" asks Gez
"That would be nice, love" replies Kate

(Smiling)
Gez goes over to the Bar area, and bumps into Tony …
"Well Tony, how are you getting on?" asks Gez
"Oh, like a house on fire" laughs Tony
"Are you OK with Kate?" asks Tony
"Well, I'm getting the full life story … if you know what I mean" replies Gez
"Yea, but do you think she fancies you?" asks Tony
"It's hard to tell" replies Gez

The door of the Church Hall opens … Jane and Lucy from York enter …

"Well, hello Gez … we meet again" advises Jane
"Yea … like an old husband and wife meeting again" replies Gez (Both laugh)
"Would you like to have a drink with me?" asks Jane (Big Smile)
"Well, I'm kind of …" replies Gez
"Kind of what, darling?" asks Jane
"Oh, I see … entertaining another lady … pretty isn't she" advises Jane
"Well, maybe later then … if you can find the time" explains Jane

"Don't go Jane" asks Gez (Looks anxious)
"I'll be with you in a minute ... I'll make my excuses" advises Gez
"OK, darling ... if that's what you want?" replies Jane (Smiles)
Gez takes a drink over to Kate, then makes his excuses and leaves.
The DJ is now playing summer party hits ...
Tony looks over and begins to have a word with Gez.
"Are you OK, Gez?" asks Tony
"Oh, yea ... I'm just going to have a dance with Jane" replies Gez (Smiling)
"What about Kate?" asks Tony

"Oh it's OK ... looks like she's chatting to someone else now" advises Tony

"Sorry ... but it's not love at first sight" explains Gez
Jane returns, after powdering her nose, and is in the mood for dancing.
"Jane, where is that dance floor" asks Gez
"Come on darling ... let's get into the groove" replies Jane
Another Tuesday Bar Night follows at Tapas in Leeds.
Gez is talking to someone he's known for a while at the bottom of the stairs up to the next level. A girl with long dark hair approaches. Both decide to move to one side to let her pass.
"It's OK love, we'll let you through" advises Gez

(Smiles)

"What if I don't want to go through?" replies the young lady (Big Smile)

Gez puts his arms around her waist ...
"OK, stay with me then, love" replies Gez (Smiles)

"Have you met ... sorry what's your name?" asks Gez

"Charlotte" replies the young lady
But, I remembered the Zodiac code, and I thought I didn't want to end up as a "ship passing in the night" and so I let Charlotte go back amongst all the other members.
Gez was polite about the whole thing!

NO MAN IS AN ISLAND!

A word in your shell like! A pep talk from Mike, but even he falls foul of his own advice!
Sovereign Street, Leeds, Tuesday, 7.30pm.

Gez parks his car and begins to walk towards Tapas, but bumps into a work colleague en route!
"Hey ... fancy meeting you here"
advises Gez (Laughing)
"Yea, I'm just on my way home"
replies Pat
"Fancy a swift half before you go?" asks Gez
"Where are you going?" asks Pat
"I'm on my way to Zodiac, at Tapas" replies Gez "Zodiac?" asks Pat (Looks surprised)
"Come on Pat, lets have that drink ... I'll tell you all about it over a beer" explains Gez
Gez and Pat walk down Sovereign Street towards a pub near the traffic lights.
They enter the Bridge Pub ...

"Right, I'll order ... you find a seat" advises Pat

"What are you having?" asks Pat
(Points to Bar)
"Oh, just a coke for me ... I'm driving" replies Gez

"Yea, me too … just a small one for me, too" advises Pat

"Coming right up" advises Pat
"OK mate, see you in a jiffy" replies Gez

Pat goes over to the bar, and orders a couple of beers …
"I'd like a coke and a small beer, please" asks Pat
 The Bar woman takes the order
…
"No worries, mate" (man's voice)

Pat seems to be ages at the bar … then suddenly returns …

"Everything OK, Pat?" asks Gez (Looks concerned)
"No, far from it" replies Pat (Looks stunned)

"You look very pale … as if you've seen a ghost?" asks Gez

"You know where we are … don't you?" asks Pat
"Yea, we're in a pub in Leeds" replies Gez (smiling)
"Not just any pub, mate" advises Pat
"Oh?" asks Gez (Looks puzzled)

"This is a gay bar" replies Pat (Looks shocked)

"It's OK, Pat … just chill"

replies Gez (laughing)

"Your very cool about it" adds
Pat
"Don't worry, no one will bother us"
replies Gez (laughing)
"OK, tell me more about Zodiac" asks
Pat
"Well" advises Gez (both laughing)

Zodiac is a singles based organisation with branches all over the UK. It's prime directive, is to bring together single people, from all walks of life. It also provides social activities in a relaxed atmosphere. It is run by the members.
The interior of Tapas Bar has a plush seating and standing area. The DJ section and dance floor is to the left. Tapas is located in Lower Briggate, Leeds.

8pm close to the Bar area. A pep talk from Mike, but even he falls foul of his own advice!
"No man is an island" advises
Mike (Smiling)
"That's Shakespeare" explains
Mike (Still smiling)
"I don't follow, Mike?" replies
Gez (Looks puzzled)
"Well, Single man in Leeds … away from home … lots of temptations … we all react in different ways" advises Mike
"We do?" asks Gez (Still looks puzzled)

"Oh yea … well for me, it was stamp collecting" explains Mike (Laughing)

"Is this a wind up?" asks Gez (Laughing)

"No, don't laugh … but it really was kind of soothing" advises Mike (Smiling)

"We all need a time, when we're on our own" explains Mike
"Really?" replies Gez (Laughing)

"This is a wind up" laughs Gez (Both Laughing)

"No, listen to what Mike is saying to you … it's sound advice" replies Ernest

"Oh, I will, Ernest … I will" replies Gez (Smiling)
"The solution whatever it is, wherever it is, lies with you … it has to" explains Mike (Looking serious)
"What the heck are you on about, Mike?" asks Gez (Smiling)
"Well, you've got quite a following here" advises Mike
"A following?" asks Gez
(Looks puzzled)
"The fair sex" laughs Ernest
"The best thing is, that you don't really know it … do you?" asks Mike
"Well" replies Gez (Still puzzled)
"Oh, you seem to be a hit with all the ladies on Bar nights, and at parties" explains Mike (Smiling)
"What if I am?" asks Gez (Looks embarrassed)

"Oh, yea … I've noticed it too"
replies Ernest
"And me too" replies Tony
(Laughing)
"Hi Tony … have you just arrived?" asks Gez

"Yea, only just … listen to Mike's very sound advice, mate" replies Tony

"Now, where was I?" asks Mike (Scratching his head)

"A hit with the ladies?" replies Gez (Still stunned)

"Well, it's true … you've got quite a following here" advises Mike

"Are you pulling my leg?" asks Gez
"No … straight up" replies Mike

"Well, maybe I'm fond of one or two, but I can assure you that I won't step out of line" adds Gez (Looks concerned)
"We, know that lad" advises Ernest (Smiling)

"I won't step out of character, either" replies Gez

"Remember the little Sharon and Adam incident, and ships passing in the night?" asks Gez
"Oh, that was different,
Gezza" replies Mike
"I've heard them saying …"
advises Mike
"Saying what?" asks Gez
(Looks very concerned)
"That you play it close" explains Mike (Look serious)

"Your a kind of enigma … they can't work you out, lad" advises Ernest

"And?" asks Mike (Smiling)
"Go on" asks Gez (Looks stunned)

"Have you been questioned about your love life?" asks Mike (Still smiling)

"My love life?" asks Gez (Looks serious)
"There's no one … that's the plain truth" explains Gez

"I'm flattered … but for now all I need is the here and now, and to be well … socially active" advises Gez
"You don't have a portrait of yourself in the attic do you?" asks Ernest (Looks serious)
"Of course not" replies Gez (Smiling)
"There are no skeletons in the cupboard, either" explains Gez (Laughs)

"I will admit that there are certain ladies on the radar, but it's like being in a sweet shop … so many choices but which one to choose?" adds Gez

"We're all a bit like that, Gezza" advises Tony
"You never know until you've tried" adds Ernest (Smiling)
"Thanks for the advice, mate" replies Gez (Laughs)
"Well, he's right on that one" advises Mike
"Go on lad, fill your boots" laughs Ernest

"Any road, I've got three smashers lined up for afters" advises Mike … Everyone is laughing …
"Have you?" asks Gez, looking puzzled

Yea, two blondes, and don't look so worried, they've got their Mother with them" replies Mike (Everyone in Tapas laughing)
"Oh, that's OK then" replies Ernest (Looks suspicious)

"I'm glad you think so … she's

yours" replies Mike

Lots of Laughing

"We're all behaving like little boys ... easily led" replies Gez (Smiles)

"You said it, Gezza" replies Mike, both laughing

"Your a proper Johnny Know all Mike, but I guess, you already know that?" advises Ernest, laughing

"Ernest ... coming from you, I'm not sure if that's supposed to be a compliment or not?" replies Mike (Everyone laughing)

"It's just a joke, Ernest ... we've all met them before" advises Gez

Mike pulls Gez to one side ...

"Where was I?" asks Mike (Looks serious)

"You were telling me that I was on a lot of girls radar?" replies Gez

"Why aren't you pulling?" asks Mike (Smiles)
"I'm not resisting anyone, Mike ... you've got it all wrong" advises Gez (Smiling)

"Well, go on then smarty pants, why are you giving them the brush off?" asks Mike (Lots of Laughter)
"What a question to ask" replies a lady in the background

"I'm not giving them the brush off either, Mike ... I love all girls" replies Gez

"Well, we've noticed your a little coy ... there's a lot of crumpet lining up ... and it's all on a plate"

advises Mike (More Laughter)
"Crumpet … don't worry, I like my girls full on … know what I mean?" replies Gez
"I've seen you mooning over one or two … go on lad, your ships come in" advises Mike (Lots of Laughing)
"Listen to what Mike is telling you … it's sound advice" replies Ernest (Smiles)
"He knows what he's talking about" explains Ernest (Laughs)
"You've got them all in a lather, Gezza … they are all gagging for it" advises Mike
"Well, whatever it is, it lies with you" explains Mike
"You've got quite a following here … and you don't really know it" says Ernest (Lots of Laughing)
"OK, Mike … I'll try to assert myself, are you happy now?" replies Gez
"Good lad … consider yourself initiated, into the Mike book of pulling" advises Mike (Laughs)
"Go, get them, tiger" laughs Ernest (Laughing)

"Good on you, Gezza … Mike's right, they are gagging for it" explains Ernest (All Laughing)

Tony enters the bar area (He is in his mid fifties, clean shaven, cynical)

"Yes, Ernest's right … that little blonde, at the weekend … it was on a plate" advises Tony (Laughing)
"You missed out there, big time, Gezza … she was a real cracker too" explains Tony
"Thanks for your take on the matter, Tony" replies Gez

"Mike's an authority on crumpet ... he speaks the truth" advises Tony (Lots of laughing)

"Now, where was I?" asks Mike (Everyone Laughing)
"I think, I'm taking all of this pretty well, don't you?" asks Gez (Looks stunned)

"A hit with the ladies ... Mike's guide to crumpet pulling?" advises Gez (All Laughing)

"That's it Gezza ... glad to hear that you were listening" laughs Mike
"Oh yea ... well it's true you've got quite a following here, and Ernest and Tony are right, they are gagging for it" advises Mike (Smiling)
"All you need to do is get their attention first ... then get into their knickers ... not necessarily in that order" explains Mike
(Lots more Laughter)

"Very funny, Mike"
replies Gez

"Are you pulling my
leg?" asks Gez
"No, straight up ... and I'm not pulling your plonker either" adds Mike (Everyone now in stitches at Mike's question and answer section)
"So come on Gezza, stop being so naive" advises Mike
"Remember the little Sharon/Adam incident ... and ships passing in the night?" asks Gez (Looking serious)
"Oh, that was different ... they are all after your

body, big time" explains Mike
"After my body ... are they all sex maniacs?" replies Gez
(Lots of laughing)

"It's better than being in the audience at the Leeds City Varieties" quips Tony (More laughter)
"Well, if they are, let me have some of it ... go on dip your toe in the water and see how it goes" replies Mike
(More Laughing)

"OK, Mike, I'll take your advice" advises Gez

"I knew, sooner or later, you'd see the error of your ways" quips Mike (More Laughing)
"No time like the present" advises Mike

"What do you make of the little blonde and her mate, at the Bar?" asks Mike

"They look to be a couple of stunners ... nicely put together" replies Gez (Smiling)

"Come on Gezza, I'll show you how the master does it" advises Mike (Pointing)
"OK, Mike ... let's go for
it" replies Gez (Everyone
Laughing)
"Crumpet dead ahead ... this one's nailed on" advises Mike (Laughing)
"OK, Mike ... I'm right behind you" replies Gez (Laughing)
"Don't keep all those lovely ladies waiting" advises Ernest

"They are all lining up for you ... lucky sods" explains Ernest
"OK, Ernest ... now watch closely" replies Gez (Laughing)
"Go on, take the plunge ... go for it" advises Tony
"You never know, until you've tried ... and I like to try before I buy" quips Ernest
"Thanks for the advice, mate ... I'll remember what you said" replies Gez (Smiling)
"Well, he's right on this one, Gezza ... they are virtually ours for the taking" replies Mike
"Go on lad, fill your boots, time waits for no man" advises Ernest
"I'm a semi retired sex maniac" explains Ernest
(Everyone Laughing)

Gez, checks the Notice Board, and see that there is yet another party in York at the weekend ...
"Does anyone put parties on in Leeds, and when is the next one?" asks Gez
"Oh, they'll come up lad ... just keep an eye on the board" advises Ernest
"All those ladies are begging for it" explains Ernest
"Are we talking parties or something else, Ernest?" answers Gez (Laughing)
"You stink of yesterday's booze, Ernest" advises Mike (Smiling)
"It was a bit of a blinder yesterday, Mike" replies

Ernest (Smiling)

"Well, Gezza … what have you found on the notice board?" asks Mike

"Ah here's one … a party at the Rose of York pub on Saturday … and to contact Jane and Lucy for tickets" advises Gez

"Hey, your in there … they can have my body for nothing" replies Ernest (Everyone Laughing)

"Am I?" asks Gez

(Looking puzzled)

"You, know you are"

replies Mike

"Don't tell me, they are both gagging

for it too?" asks Gez (Lots of Laughter)

"They like you … no harm in that … and if they are gagging for it … go and get them" quips Ernest (Everyone Laughing)

"Ernest, your sex mad … and yes I've noticed, they both have lovely bodies" replies Gez (Smiling)

"Go on lad … opportunity knocks … go and knock them off" quips Ernest (All Laughing)

"Talk of the devil … here they are" advises Tony (Points to door)

Jane and Lucy enter Tapas Bar area. Jane is slim, attractive, has short brunette hair, and wearing the fashions of the day. Lucy is also slim, has shoulder length blonde hair, again very attractive … both are in their mid forties …

"We were just talking about you"

advises Tony (Smiling)

"Were you, darling, I hope it was all bad" laughs Jane
"Naturally" advises Mike (All Laughing)
"How are you both tonight … you look stunning" quips Mike (Smiling)
"Oh, fine and dandy … your such a charmer, Mike" replies Lucy (Big Smile)
"We're here to sell our tickets" advises Jane
Gez moves forward to greet Jane and Lucy …
"Now you want one darling, don't you?" asks Jane (Big Smile)
"How can I say, No, to you, Jane?" asks Gez (Smiles back)
"Oh, some have, but you won't your smitten, aren't you?" asks Jane
Gez looks really embarrassed and quite sheepish …
"Well I …" replies Gez (still looking very embarrassed)
"What's the matter, Gez … cat got your tongue, darling?" asks Jane
"You know me, Jane" replies Gez (Looks stunned)
"You should know all about … female intuition, darling" explains Jane
(Everyone Laughing)
"I think I'm getting to know yours" advises Gez
"If it's any help … I'm smitten with you too, darling"

replies Jane (Sexy Wink)

"Jane, you say the most wonderful things" replies Gez (Looking well and truly gobsmacked)
"See what we mean?" asks Mike (Eggs Gez on)

"It's nailed on … go get them, cowboy" explains Mike (Everyone Laughing)
"Yee ahh … go on lad … she won't wait for ever … I'd make her weak at the knees" quips Ernest (Lots of Laughing)
The DJ is now playing Donna Summer's Hot Stuff …

"Come on Gez, time for a dance … Lucy you come too … and drag Tony on the floor" asks Jane (Smiling)
"Go on, Gez … and remember what I told you … no man is an island" advises Mike
"OK, Jane, you've convinced me, lets start grooving" asks Gez
"You look hot stuff, tonight" advises Gez (Smiling)
"Well, thank you, kind Sir" replies Jane (Beaming)

"Well, they can have my body for nothing" advises Ernest (Lots of Laughing)

"So you keep saying, mate … but are they really turned on?" asks Mike (Smirking)
"I know how to push their buttons" quips Ernest (Lots of Laughing)
"Ernest, you never fail to amaze me" replies Mike (All Laughing)

THE LIFE AND SOUL
OF THE PARTY

Saturday morning, Headingley shopping centre … Gez is wandering down the street, heading towards his car, with lots of shopping bags …
Two elderly ladies are having early morning coffee at a roadside Cafe …
"Isn't that?" advises the first Lady (Looks shocked)
"Who?" asks the second Lady (Peering)
"I'm sure it was him" replies the first Lady

Gez suddenly disappears from view, but was he recognised, and more importantly, has his cover been blown?
Who is Gez?
Why is he hiding a secret?

The Rose of York Pub, outskirts of York, early Saturday evening … approx 8pm in the Private Function Suite … a Zodiac members only event …
Mike, Gez, Ernest and Tony have just turned up … Jane greets them at the door
"Hi … thank you for coming to our event" advises Jane (Smiling)
"It's our pleasure, love" advises Mike

"We're only here for the beer" explains Mike (Laughing)

"Well, not all of us, Mike" replies Gez (Looks embarrassed)

"I'm on the pull" advises Ernest (Everyone Laughing)

"Sorry, Jane … he's already had one or two" replies Tony (Smiles)
"I'm alright, lad … I didn't do it ossifer" laughs Ernest (Lots of Laughing)
Everyone enters, the now almost full, function suite.
Jane decides to go in for the kill, and springs a surprise on Gez.
"Gotcha … where I want you at last" advises Jane (Smiling)
"Looks like you have, Jane" replies Gez (Looks embarrassed)
"Well, have you missed me?" asks Jane
"Oh, I always miss you, Jane, you know that" replies Gez (Arm around Jane)
"I'm glad to hear it, darling" advises Jane (Sexy wink)
"You and Lucy are the life and soul …" replies Gez
"… of the party" quips Mike (All Laughing)
"Where have you been?" asks Gez
"Oh, checking out the bar … and the talent" replies Mike (Laughing)
"Why don't you come and join us?" asks Jane

"You know what, I'll come and join you" replies Mike (Laughing)
"OK, by me, Mike" advises Lucy (Big Smile)
Jane, Lucy, Gez and Mike take to the dance floor.

After a few dances, Gez and Mike retreat to the bar, for a breather. Ernest and Tony take over.
"We'll be back, honey ... I need a rest" advises Mike (Looks serious)
"Are you OK, Mike?" asks Gez (Looks concerned)
"Have I worn you both out already?" asks Jane

"Oh, we'll be back honey ... now keep everything nice and warm" advises Gez

"Only for you, darling ... only for you" replies Jane (Everyone Laughing)
Meanwhile, at the Bar in the function room at the Rose of York Pub ...
"Wow, it's great to have a breather, Mike" advises Gez
"Oh yea, I needed it, Gezza" replies Mike (Laughing)

Mike orders the beers, and they both catch up on various matters ...

"Well, how did you get on last weekend?" asks Gez
"Oh, I made a mistake, mate ... big time" replies Mike (Looks serious)
"Why ... what happened?" asks Gez (Looks puzzled)
"Well, I gave into temptation" replies

Mike (Looks serious)
"Yea, but I thought that's what you wanted?" advises Gez
"Remember, Wanda?" asks Mike
"What about, Wanda?" asks Gez
(Looks puzzled)
"Well, I kind of …" replies Mike (Winking)
"Oh, now I get the picture" advises Gez (Laughing)

"I know I shouldn't have … but I couldn't stop myself" replies Mike

"Your only human, Mike" assures Gez
"Don't worry, your secret's safe with me … and the book of crumpet pulling too" replies Gez (Lots of Laughing)
"I see Jane's got her eye on you tonight, Gezza" advises Mike (Looks intrigued)

"What can I say … she's got terrific taste" replies Gez (Both Laughing)

"I fancy my chances with Lucy" advises Mike
"Well, go for it" replies Gez

"Your a good mate Gez, there's something I've been meaning to ask you" advises Mike (Looks serious)
"Go on, what is it Mike?" asks Gez (Looks anxious)

"I could do with some help at Tapas bar nights" replies Mike

"Do you want me to help you, Mike?"

asks Gez

"Are you up for it?" asks Mike

"Sure, Mike … count me in … I'll do it" replies Gez

"You do know that you'll become even more popular with the ladies, don't you?" asks Mike (Both Laughing)

"OK, that's fine with me … now tell me more about Wanda" explains Gez
Meanwhile Rick from Huddersfield turns up, and Mike's not happy …
"Watch your back, just look who's rolled up" advises Mike (Looks serious)
"Who?" asks Gez (Looks around)
"Rick from Huddersfield … now he is a funny guy" advises Mike
"I take it, you don't mean as in … ha ha?" replies Gez
"Got it in one … no one likes that bloke … total nob head" advises Mike (Everyone Laughing)
"Some do" replies Gez

"Yea, you'll be surprised, he has his followers" explains Mike

"I'm not one of them" advises Mike
"Nor am I" replies Gez (Both Laughing)

Gez starts to tell Mike about the last New Year's Eve Party in Huddersfield …

"He's brain dead, a real tosser" advises Mike
"Just forget about him, Mike" replies Gez
"He'll not get in our way" explains Mike
"That's for sure" advises Gez
"If he does, he'll wish he hadn't" advises Mike (Looks serious)
"OK, Mike … take it easy" replies Gez

(Calms Mike down)
Tony and Ernest arrive back
at the bar …
"I'm all in … I'm worn out"
advises Ernest
"We're just getting started, Ernest"
replies Tony (Laughing)
"Has he behaved himself tonight?"
asks Mike (Laughing)
"Yes, he's been a good lad …
"Jane and Lucy have been asking about you two"
advises Tony
"Well, I suppose they can have my body for nothing" replies Mike (Laughing)
"Come on Gezza … our work is never done" explains Mike (Lots of Laughing)
The next party, was also in York, at a Hotel opposite the Race course …
Main Function Room … Saturday evening, approx 8.30pm … Nick (Mid fifties, distinguished, handsome)
Tony and Gez decide to attend …

"Hi, nice to see you both … glad you could make it" advises Nick (Smiling)

"Oh, it's our pleasure, Nick … we're looking for some fun tonight" replies Tony

"We always love coming to York … and delving deeply into it's treasures" advises Gez (All Laughing)
"Well, good evening boys … start delving now … fun this way" advises Jane

"Hi Jane … well go on then … show me the funny" asks Tony
"Hi Jane" replies Gez (Smiling)

"You did say funny didn't you?" asks Jane

"You both look great tonight" explains Jane
"Yea, fanny later … we didn't want to let you down" replies Tony (All Laughing)
"Your looking quite elegant tonight, Jane" advises Gez
"Everything is nice and tight, in the right places" explains Gez
Jane looks quite seductive!
"Oh, this old thing … I only wear it, when I don't care what people think" replies Jane (Sexy or what?)
"Yes, I bet" replies Gez (Laughing)

"Lucy looks quite the picture too" advises Tony (She looks stunning)

"Two stunners" explains Tony
"Oh, here come Dee and Kate, Tony" advises Gez
Both look really attractive and work their charm on Tony …
"I think Dee's keen on you, Tony" explains Gez
"Yes, I know" replies Tony (Smiling)

Tony and Dee decide to go for a drink at the bar …

"I'm just going with Dee, for a drink, see you later Gezza" advises Tony (Points to Bar)

"See you later, Tony" replies Gez (Smiles)
The DJ starts to play the Zodiac anthem … SIMPLY THE BEST by TINA TURNER …
"Come on everyone … all on the dance floor" shouts Nick
All the party revellers take to the dance floor, which is now full to capacity.
"That goes for you too, honey … come on" advises Jane (Sexy wink)
"You really are looking radiant tonight, Jane" advises Gez

"Well, thank you kind Sir?" replies Jane (Big Smile)

"Are you trying to get into my knickers?" asks Jane (Big Smile)

"What a thing to say" replies Gez (Smiling)

"What do you think Jane?" adds Gez (Laughing)
"I think your quite a charmer, and you have a way with women" replies Jane
"Thank you, pretty lady" responds Gez (Smiling)
"But there is something about you, that doesn't add up?" advises Jane
"What do you mean, Jane?" asks Gez (Looks puzzled)
"Female intuition, darling" replies Jane (Smiling)

"You seem to be protecting, or hiding something" explains Jane (Looks puzzled)

"Am I, well if I am, it's only make believe"

replies Gez (Smiling)

"I wonder?" asks Jane (Smiling)
Gez and Jane retreat to the bar, where they rejoin Lucy, who is talking to Mike …
"So, you two, how are both you getting on?" asks Jane (Smiling)
"Like a house on fire, love" replies Mike (Laughing)
"Are you coming to my party, next week, Mike?" asks Lucy (Smiling)
"Party, we didn't know you were having
a party" replies Mike (Smiles)
"I'm having a decorating party next
Saturday" replies Lucy
"A decorating party?" replies Gez (Looks intrigued)

"Oh, yea … well it's redecorating my loo, actually" laughs Lucy

"Your loo?" asks Mike (Laughing)
"Yes, Mike … my loo" laughs Lucy (Smiling)

"Well, anything for a party, I suppose" advises Gez (Laughing)

"You can write on the walls, with marker pens, when you arrive" explains Lucy

"Well, Gezza … are you up for it?" asks Mike (Laughing)
"Sounds to be right up my street … get it
… write" laughs Gez
"If I were you, I'd stick to your day job" replies Mike (Laughing)
"Why?" asks Gez

"Well, if ever comedy makes a come back, we'll get you on Leeds City Varieties" advises Mike (Everyone Laughing)
"You've both got to come"
advises Jane (Big Smile)
"OK, your on, we'll be there, love"
replies Mike
"You can write on the walls … Gez loves Jane … can't you darling?" asks Jane (Sexy wink)
"Well, I might do, you never know"
replies Gez (Laughing)
"Here comes, Tony and Dee" advises Mike
"Are you both coming to my decorating the loo party, next Saturday?" asks Lucy
"Decorating the Loo?" replies Tony (Looks stunned)
"We'll be there"
advises Dee
"Where and when?"
asks Tony

DECORATING THE LOO PARTY

Saturday night, Lucy's decorating the loo party, on the outskirts of York. Lucy's lounge/bar area … lots of ladies/music blaring in the background … Tony and Gez arrive on the scene and are greeted by Lucy …
"Hi Tony and Gez … thanks for coming to my party" advises Lucy (Big smile)
"It's our pleasure, love … where's Jane?" asks Gez (Looks around)
"Bottles and plates, over there" explains Lucy (Pointing)
"Mines, the bulls blood wine" advises
Tony (Laughing)
"OK Tone … your booze is stashed" replies Gez (Laughing)
"Jane's over there Gez … she's been waiting for you" advises Lucy (Points)

Gez wanders over to Jane and puts his arm around her waist …

"Hi Jane, you look nicely put together tonight" advises Gez (Very tasty)

"You're not so bad yourself, honey" replies Jane (Sexy Wink)
"I've written something on Lucy's loo wall" advises Gez (Smiling)

"Well, what did you write, darling?" asks Jane

"Oh, I put ... madly ... deeply ... about you of course" replies Gez (Smiling)

"Your a bit of a dark horse, aren't you darling?" asks Jane (Looks puzzled)

"Dark horse?" asks Gez (Looks cautious)

"There's something about you that doesn't quite fit" replies Jane

"What have you been thinking?" asks Gez (Now on his guard)

"Just a feeling ... I can't explain it" replies Jane

"Are you psychic?" asks Gez (Smiling)

"Maybe, but you've got nothing to worry about, honey" adds Jane

"Besides, flattery will get you everywhere, darling" explains Jane (Laughing)

We meet Chris, near the bar, a fireman from Huddersfield. He is also not a Rick fan!

"Hi, I'm Gez ... this is Jane" advises Gez (Both shaking hands with Chris)

"Hi, I'm Chris, a new member from Huddersfield" advises Chris (Smiling)

"I'm just going to powder my nose, love" advises Jane (Big Smile)

"OK, Jane see you soon" replies Gez (Smiling)

Tony joins Gez at the bar and also meets Chris ...

"Chris this is Tony ... we're both from

Leeds" advises Gez Chris is in his late thirties, attractive, good humoured … "Nice to meet you … it's my first event" advises Chris

"Well, how's things at Huddersfield bar night? asks Gez
"Oh, lots of nice people … except for one" replies Chris (Looks mad)
"We know exactly who you mean" replies Gez
"Now, let me guess" explains Gez (Laughing)
"Yea, me too" advises Tony (More Laughing)
"Does he go by the name of, Rick?" asks Gez
"As in prick?" replies Tony (Lots of Laughing)
"Yes, that's the guy" advises Chris (More Laughing)

"We, can't stand the man … well we think it's a man" advises Gez

"But, we can't really be sure" adds Tony (Lots of Laughing)
"Oh, he thinks he's some sort of Casanova" explains Chris

"Never seen him with a woman, have you, Tony?" asks Gez (Laughing)

"No, never, Gezza" replies Tony (Laughing)
"Well lets face it, no woman would want to be seen dead with him" adds Chris

"You said it mate" replies Gez (Laughing)
"Looks like, we're all on the same wavelength" replies Chris (Laughing)
"Chris, come to Leeds bar night, on Tuesday ... we promise to look after you" advises Gez
"Why, are there lots of women there?" asks Chris (Looks intrigued)
"You'll be spoilt for choice" advises Tony (Laughing)
Jane, suddenly arrives on the scene, looking very seductive ...

"I've been looking for you, where have you been?" asks Jane (Big Smile)

Gez pulls Jane towards him, and puts his arms around her waist.
"Oh, just chatting ... Jane this is Chris ... he's new to Zodiac" advises Gez (Smiling)

"Well hello, darling ... where have you been all my life?" replies Jane (Laughing)

"Well, I'm really speechless Jane" responds Chris (All Laughing)
"Oh, you'll soon get used to Jane ... she's one of our girls" advises Gez (Laughing)
Lucy now enters the scene, and is taken in by Tony ...
 "Only, one of your girls?" asks Lucy (Big Smile)
"Sorry, Chris ... this is Lucy ... another one of our girls" explains Gez (Laughing)

"You know what, I think I'm going to like Zodiac" replies Chris (Laughing)
"You and me, both mate" replies Tony (All Laughing)
"Don't forget about me" adds Gez (All Laughing)
"All for one … and one for all" add Tony/Gez and Chris (Laughing)

Gez quizzes Jane and Lucy, and asks if they intend to go to the Leeds Christmas dance …
"Well, are you both going to the Zodiac Dinner dance at the Queens Hotel?" asks Gez (Smiling)
"Oh, yea … we've got our tickets" advises Jane/Lucy (Smiling)
"What about you, darling?" asks Jane (Winking)

"We'll be there too … so expect some surprises" advises Tony (Laughing)

"What surprises?" asks Jane (Looks puzzled)
"Well, if we tell you now, it wouldn't be a surprise, darling … would it?" replies Gez
"Your a real dark horse" advises Jane (Smiling)
"Nay" replies Gez (All Laughing)
"We'll come up with something, on the night" explains Tony (Laughing)
"Are you both going?" asks Gez
"Yes of course, we'll be there … we told you, we've already got our tickets" replies Jane/Lucy (Sexy Winking)
"What about you Chris?" asks Tony

"Oh, I'll have to check to see if I'm not on then ... but hopefully, I'll be there" advises Chris
"OK, Chris ... come to Leeds bar night on Tuesday" advises Gez
"I'm the new Meet and Greeter with Mike" explains Gez
"When did that happen?" asks Tony (Looks puzzled)
"Oh, only recently ... Mike needs some help" advises Gez (Laughing)

The DJ changes the mood on the dance floor to classic love songs ...

"Now where's my smooch ... you know you promised me, darling" advises Jane

"Looks like your in tonight" advises Tony (Laughing)
"OK, darling ... I'm coming" replies Gez (All Laughing)
Tapas Wine Bar, the following Tuesday, approx. 8.30pm ...
Gez talks to Mike and they catch up on the previous weekend's events ...
"Hey up, Gezza ... well how did it go at the weekend?" asks Mike (Laughing)
"It was great, Mike ... Tony and I went to Lucy's decorating the loo party in York" replies Gez (More Laughing)
"Decorating the Loo ... you are having me on, right?" asks Mike (Laughing)
"No, mate ... it's the truth" replies Gez (Laughing)
"Glad I didn't go to that one ... any excuse for a wee

up, get it?" asks Mike (Laughing)

"Oh yea, I was totally pickled" replies Gez (Laughing)

"Well, Mike … you missed a bobby dazzler" explains Gez (Laughing)

"What about the talent … tell me about the talent" asks Mike (More Laughing)

In walks, man about town, Ernest, dressed to kill …

"Well, did I miss anything at the weekend?" asks Ernest
"You didn't get your knickers in a twist did you?" explains Ernest (All Laughing)

"No, on the contrary … in fact I was surprised that you weren't there, Ernest" advises Gez
"Well, I did think about it … but my pecker wasn't working" quips Ernest
"Pecker?" asks Gez (Laughing)
"Don't ask" replies Mike (Laughing)

Tony arrives at Tapas, followed by new member, Chris …

"Welcome Tony and Chris … glad to see you both in Leeds" advises Gez

"Two new ladies have arrived … I'll take care of this Gezza" replies Mike
"Smooth operator … no doubt more for the Mike book of pulling" explains Gez (Laughing)
"Well, I'm impressed" advises Chris (Big smile)

"The surroundings are intimate … nice dance floor … nice bar area" explains Chris (Smiling)

"What about the ladies?" asks Tony (Laughing)

"You've both been true to your word ... lots of them here tonight" replies Chris

"You'll be spoilt for choice, Chris" advises Gez (Laughing)
"Just like us" replies Tony (Lots of Laughing)

"A word of warning to the wise, though" advises Gez (Looks Serious)

"Go on" replies Chris (Listening intently)
"Don't let everyone know your business ... know what I mean ... people talk here?" explains Gez (Wink Wink)
"Gotcha in one ... don't worry, I'll be very discreet" replies Chris
"Good lad, we knew you would understand" advises Tony (Laughing)
Mike returns after chatting to the two new female members ...

"Well, that's two more on the radar ... they are going into the book" advises Mike (Laughing)
"I guess they come up to your standard, Mike ... right?" asks Gez (Laughing)
"Got it in one, Gezza ... they are right up my street" replies Mike (Lots of Laughing)
Gez introduces Chris to Mike ...

"Mike, this is Chris ... he's new tonight ... any advice to pass on?" asks Gez

"Where are you from, Chris?" asks Mike
"Huddersfield" replies Chris

"That's prick ... I mean Rick country" advises Mike (Everyone Laughing)

"Yea, he knows, we've already told Chris ... and he knew about him anyway" advises Gez (All Laughing)
"Good lad ... consider yourself initiated into the Leeds bar night" explains Mike
"Have a look at the Events board and make a note of any parties coming up" advises Gez (Laughing)
"Yea, Chris ... we mostly go to the parties arranged by members in their homes explains Tony (Laughing)
"That's right, Tony ... but remember we do go to some bigger venues too, and we are a nationwide organisation" advises Gez
Lucy and Jane arrive at Tapas, entering the Bar area ...

"Good evening, ladies" greets Mike (Eyes popping out of their sockets)

"Hello, Mike ... how are you?" asks Lucy (Looks sexy)
"Such a charmer" replies Jane (Looks stunning)
Jane moves over to Gez and kisses him on the cheek ...

"Have you come round, Gez ... after our fling on Saturday night, darling?" asks Jane (Winking)
"Did you have a fling with Gezza?" asks Mike (Laughing)

"Oh, you should have seen them ... they were all over

IT'S A KIND OF LOVE

each other" replies Tony (Smiling)

"Lucky sod" advises Mike (Everyone Laughing)
"No, that's not entirely true,
Mike" replies Gez
"Gez is a bit of a dark horse"
explains Jane
"How come?" asks Mike (Looks
suspicious)
"Well, he's a man of mystery … no one knows where he came from, or anything about him" advises Jane
"We're all a bit like that love" replies Mike

"It's alright, Gezza … we don't kiss and tell at Zodiac" explains Mike (Reassuring)

"Any road, I hope you didn't let me down with Jane, remember what I told you?" asks Mike (Laughing)
"Yea, I remember … no man is an island"
replies Gez (Laughing)
"That's it mate, spot on" advises Mike
(Laughing)
"Well, did you rise to the occasion … or what?" asks Ernest (Laughing)
"What a question, to ask" replies Gez (Looks stunned)
"Come on, don't be shy now" advises Tony (Laughing)

"Well, don't keep us in suspenders … did you?"
asks Mike (Laughing)

"No, he bloody well didn't … leave my Gez

98

alone" replies Jane (Everyone Laughing)
"You are in there, lad" quips Ernest (All Laughing)
The DJ starts to play several upbeat 80s pop songs …
Jane pulls Gez on to the dance floor …
"Come on, darling … lets' get on the dance floor … they are playing our song?" advises Jane (Big Smile)
"They are?" asks Gez (Looks surprised)

"Saved by the bell" explains Gez (Laughs)

Mike, Ernest and Tony continue their conversation, at the bar …

"Well, if that's not an omen … I don't know what is" advises Mike (Laughing)

"I'm glad for Gez, he's a nice lad" replies Ernest
"But there's something about him" explains Mike
"What do you mean?" asks Tony (Looks surprised)
"I get the feeling that Gez is probably more than he makes out" advises Mike
"In what way?" asks Ernest
"He's very secretive … it's as if he's hiding something" advises Mike
"I think your just being paranoid, Mike" advises Tony
"Yea, maybe I am" replies Mike (Laughs)

Lucy now moves over towards Tony …

"So, what about me … am I a good catch too?" asks Lucy (Smiling)
"Your the tops, Charlie" replies Tony

"Why Charlie … don't you like my name … Lucy?" asks Lucy (Big Smile)

"Oh, I think it's brilliant, Charlie" replies Tony (Eyes popping)
"Come on Lucy, let's join Jane and Gezza on the dance floor" advises Tony
"See, that's the way to do it" advises Ernest
"Have you got your eye on anyone tonight, Chris?" asks Mike
"Well, there's a couple of girls over there … they keep giving me the eye" advises Chris (Laughing and Winking)
"Yes, there's a lot of crumpet in here tonight" replies Mike
"Come on, lad … I'll introduce you" explains Mike (Laughs)
The DJ starts to play several Halloween type records …
"Oh, it must be an omen" advises Mike (Looks to the Heavens)

Chris and Mike make a move on two stunning ladies … a striking brunette with long dark hair and a slim blonde …
"Crumpet, dead ahead" advises Mike (Laughing)
"What about me?" asks Ernest (stunned)

"Your turn will come, Ernest … we'll ask if they've got a sister" replies Mike (Laughing)
"Thanks for that" replies Ernest (Laughing)

Sam is a brunette, she has blue eyes, and is very striking. Daisy has long blonde hair, also has blue eyes and attractive …
"Hi, ladies … I'm Mike, this is Chris … is it OK if we join you?" asks Mike (Both smiling)
"Yes, of course … I'm Sam … this is Daisy" replies Sam (Big Smile)
"Well, hello, handsome … who's your friend?" asks Daisy (Beaming)
"This is Chris … first night tonight in Leeds" replies Mike (Laughing)
"What about you, Mike?" asks Sam (Big Smile)

"Oh, I'm a meeter and greeter here" advises Mike

"My partner in crime, is Gez, he's dancing over there with Jane" explains Mike (Points to dance floor)

"So, your both hands on?" asks Daisy (Beaming)
"Well, you could say that" replies Mike (Laughing)

"This is our first night tonight, love" advises Sam (Lovely smile)

"We're looking for two Devil Women?" advises Mike (Looks raunchy)
"Well, let's see if we can tempt you both then?" replies Daisy (Big Smile)

"Are you girls going to the do at the Queen's Hotel on Saturday?" asks Chris (Smiling)

"Let's have our dance first ... we'll talk about that later" advises Daisy (Winks)
Gez moves across the dance floor with Jane ...

"I see you've got yourself on the dance floor, Mike" asks Gez (Laughing)

"Well, how could we refuse such crackers" replies Mike (Laughing)

"Flatterer" replies Sam (More Laughing)
"Yes, we've both been initiated into the Mike charm school" advise Daisy and Chris (Both Laughing)
"Consider yourselves done" replies Mike (Lots of Laughing)

Back in the bar area, long time members, Stacey and Steve are continuing to sell their last remaining tickets for the do at the Queen's ...
Stacey, mid 40s, bobbed brown hair ... happy go lucky. Steve, mid 40s, distinguished.
"How's the ticket sales?" asks Mike

"We've just got a few left now"
advises Stacey

"Oh, could I have one please?"
asks Chris
"Yes, of course mate ... I'm Steve this is Stacey" advises Steve (Smiling)
"Hello to you both, I'm new here" advises Chris

"Oh, so are we ... can we come too?" ask Daisy and Sam (Smiling)

"Yes, your lucky ... it's the last two" replies

Stacey

"So, it's game on then" advises Mike (Laughing)

"We'll all be there on Saturday" replies Chris (Laughing)

"Yea, you bet mate … and we'll punch their tickets" explains Mike (Laughing)

Gez rejoins Mike and Chris in the Bar area …

"Has Mike been looking after you?" asks Gez (Smiling)

"Oh, he's just promised to stamp our tickets, on Saturday" replies Sam (More Laughing)

"Has he now?" asks Gez (Still Laughing)

"I think Mike has more on his mind than stamping tickets, love" replies Chris (All Laughing)

"You can count on that … Mike has got them on his mind for sure" replies Gez

ZODIAC CHRISTMAS DINNER DANCE

Saturday evening, Mid December, the Queen's Hotel, Leeds. Inside the main Function Suite, approx 8.15pm …

Everyone starts to arrive, and are all greeted by Mike and Gez in the Ballroom. The Hotel is a hive of activity …

The DJ is playing various Christmas songs to get everyone in the mood.

Suddenly, Mike takes to the stage and starts to make an announcement …

"Good evening everybody … Welcome to the annual Zodiac Christmas dinner dance here at the Queen's hotel" advises Mike (Lots of applause)

"OK, if you could all look for your names on the various tables, and be seated as soon as" explains Mike (Smiling)

Mike is joined by Gez on stage …

"Yes, our three course dinner is about to be served" advises Gez

"On behalf of Zodiac Leeds, both Gez and I would like to welcome you" replies Mike (Lots of Clapping and Laughter)

David, the Yorkshire Area Administrator and Manager is also present at the prestige event.

David is in his late 40s, has dark hair, and

is a cool character …

"Hey, don't forget about me" replies David

"Sorry David … what can I say Mr Leeds is here to join us too" explains Mike (More applause)

"Thank you all … may we wish you a pleasant evening" replies Gez (Smiling)

The Waitresses are now all serving dinner … but one of them has a fall on the dance floor …

"Did you see that Waitress?" asks Mike (Looks concerned)

"Yes, poor girl" replies Gez (Surprised)

"She fell flat on her backside" advises Mike (Laughing)

"Well, I especially did … and she had such a lovely backside too" replies Ernest (Lots of Laughter)

"Thanks for your two penneth, Ernest" advises Mike (More Laughing)

"Your welcome, lad … your welcome" replies Ernest (Laughing)

"I'm just going to the bar" explains Mike (Motions)

"I'll join you" replies Gez (Moves off the table)

"It's a bit pricy in here … isn't it?" asks Mike (Checks Prices)

"Oh, yea … it's proper marked up, mate" replies Gez

Mike and Gez don't notice the Mistletoe hanging above their heads …

"Why are all you girls lining up?" asks Mike (Smiling)
"Yea, the queue for the bar is over there" replies Gez (Smiling)
"Well, look above your heads" reply Daisy and Sam (Laughing)
"Blimey, our ships come in, Gezza" replies Mike (Laughing)
Jane and Lucy enter the Bar area ...

"Gotcha, where I want you at last" advises Jane (Plants a smacker on Gez's lips)

"Thanks for that, love" replies Gez (Looks Embarrassed)
"Well, how was it for you, darling?" asks Jane (Smiling)
"Oh, absolutely first class ... lets have another" replies Gez
"Happy to help" responds Jane (Smiling)
"OK, ladies ... form a queue ... looks like you'll have to do with me" advises Mike (Laughing)
Tony and Chris arrive at the bar ...

"Don't worry Mike ... reinforcements have arrived" advises Tony (Laughing)
"OK, who's first?" asks Mike (Laughing)

The DJ starts to play a mixture of pop and Christmas songs ...

"Jane, it's time for a dance ... where's Lucy?" asks Gez (Looks around)

"Oh, it's just you and me, darling … Lucy is a big girl now" replies Jane (Smiling)

Jane and Gez get on the dance floor which is now almost full with would be Zodiac members …
"What are you doing over Christmas, Jane?" asks Gez
"Well, I'm open to offers" replies Jane (Smiling)
"Are you pulling my plonker?" asks Gez (Laughing)

"Give me time … just give me time" replies Jane (Everyone Laughing)

"Have you always been this flirty, Jane?" asks Gez (Smiling)
"Oh, it's all part of a girls make up, darling … flirting is so much fun" explains Jane (Beaming)
"Well, I'm impressed" replies Gez (All Laughing)

"Let's have a drink at the bar, honey" asks Jane (Smiling)

"Yea, let's see how Mike and Co are getting on" replies Gez (Laughing)

Jane and Gez retreat off the dance floor to find Ernest propping up the bar …

"Well, are you both having a good time?" asks Ernest
"Yes, Ernest … how are you getting on, mate?" asks Gez

"Oh, so so … always remember lad, if you haven't pulled by Midnight … there's always another day" advises Ernest (Laughing)

"Oh, I'll bear it in mind, ... I promise I will" replies Gez (Laughing)

"Hey, you've pulled here tonight, darling ... now where were we?" asks Jane (Big Smile)

"Sorry, Ernest ... duty calls" replies Gez (Laughing)

Mike comes over to talk to Jane and Gez. He looks concerned about Ernest ...

"Is he OK?" asks Mike (Looks very Concerned)

"Oh, Ernest ... I think he's had one too many" replies Gez (Laughing)

"I'm as right as nine pence" replies Ernest (Laughing)

"Oh, he'll have a corker tomorrow ... when he wakes up" advises Mike (Looks serious)

Tony and Chris retreat from the dance floor and make their way to the bar ...

"Well, are we all having a good time?" asks Tony (Laughing)

"Yes, mate ... the best" replies Gez (Laughing)

"Come on it's Christmas ... now, where's my woman?" replies Mike (Laughing)

"Are you looking for Sam?" asks Chris (Laughing)

"Yea, Sammy ... where is she?" asks Mike (Laughing)

"Here she is Mike ... she's been dancing with me and Lucy" advises Tony (Laughing)

"Yea, she's been looking for you" explains Lucy (Laughing)

"I've got a Christmas present for her"

replies Mike (Laughing)
"What is it?" asks Sam (Smiling)
"Guess?" replies Mike (Laughing)

"OK … your place or mine?" replies Sam (Sexy Wink)

"Blimey … your a fast worker love" replies Mike (Laughing)

"You said it, baby" advises Sam (All Laughing)

"Where's Ernest?" asks Gez (Very concerned)

"Oh, he's taking a breather, darling" advises Jane
"You do know that Ernest is a World War 2 veteran, don't you?" asks Mike
"No, I never knew that" replies Gez (Surprised)
"Wow" replies Tony (Looks Stunned)
"Oh, yea … he was an RAF pilot, and he took part in the Dam Buster's mission" advises Mike
"Heck … Ernest's a hero" responds Gez (Looks stunned)

"It's incredible … total respect for Ernest" advises Tony (Looks surprised)

"Yes … we should look after old Ernest" advises Mike (Looks serious)

"Ernest is one of the main stays of Zodiac" explains Mike

"I'll fetch him over … we'll never leave him on his own again" advises Gez
Going back to the Bar area … Ernest is doing what he does best … chatting up another lady …
"Hi, Ernest … are you OK, mate?" asks Gez

"I am lad … always remember, never mix business with pleasure" quips Ernest (Smiling)

Jane wanders over to the bar area …
"Ernest, come and dance with me, love" asks Jane (on Dance Floor)
"Don't mind if I do, love" replies Ernest (Smiling)
"Well, where's my Christmas kiss?" asks Ernest (Laughing)

Jane plants a smacker on Ernest …

"How's that, darling?"
asks Jane
"I'm on cloud nine, love" replies Ernest (Smiling)

Gez and Mike are deep in conversation, near the bar …

"I'll talk to David about Ernest" advises Mike
"What are you planning, Mike?" replies Gez
"A bit of a do for Ernest" replies Mike
"Yea, I think we'll arrange something special for Ernest" advises Mike

"When?" asks Gez

"I was thinking about the next bar night" explains Mike

"What do you think?" asks Mike

"Yea, I think that's a good idea, Mike" replies Gez

ERNEST'S SURPRISE PARTY

It's the Tuesday Bar night in between Christmas and New Year's Eve. Twixmas!

Inside Tapas, close to the bar area ... Mike and Gez are deep in talks about what's on the agenda, concerning Ernest's bit of a do ...
"Hi Gezza ... I've spoken to David"
advises Mike
"Was he up for it?" asks Gez
"Oh, yea ... well and truly"
explains Mike
"What did he say?" asks Gez
"David has agreed to come along later ... to present Ernest with something special" explains Mike
"What is it, Mike?" asks Gez

"We're presenting Ernest, with a Gold Card" advises Mike

"There's only six cards issued in the country" explains Mike

"What does it do for Ernest?" asks Gez
"Ernest will get special perks and he won't have to pay for membership again" advises Mike (Smiling)
"He'll also get a bottle of bubbly, and vouchers for a meal for two, at any restaurant he fancies in Leeds" replies Mike (Looks happy)
"That's fantastic ... Ernest will be well chuffed" replies Gez (Laughing)
"Yea, as I said ... only 6 Gold Cards in the country"

explains Mike (Laughing)

"Maybe one day, I'll get one?" asks Gez (and I did in July 1992 … Gold Card number 8)

"Yea, mate … maybe we'll both get one" advises Mike (Laughing)

Ernest enters Tapas, and is his usual smiling, joking self …

"Oh, Ernest's just arriving … keep tight lipped until later" advises Gez (Smiling)

"Yea … gobs tightly shut" replies Mike (Laughing)

Ernest wanders over to Mike and Gez …

"What are you two, up to?" asks Ernest (Looks puzzled)

"Nowt, mate … just getting into the Christmas spirit" advises Mike (Laughing)

"Yea, I know … whiskey, gin, brandy, vodka etc" replies Ernest (Laughing)

"Any road, are you ready for Christmas?" asks Ernest

"Why?" asks Gez (Looks surprised)

"You both look like proper turkeys" quips Ernest (Laughing)

"Gobble … gobble" replies Mike (Laughing)

"Yea, we're all set Ernest, how are you me old mate?" asks Mike (Laughing)

"Less of the old … lad" quips Ernest (More Laughing)

"Your as young as you feel, Ernest"

advises Gez (Laughing)

"Yea … and whoever you feel" quips Ernest (Lots of Laughing)

Tony enters Tapas and meanders over to talk to Mike, Gez and Ernest …

"Have I missed anything?" asks Tony (Laughing)

"No … only Ernest's usual take on life" advises Mike (All Laughing)

Chis, Jane and Lucy arrive at Tapas and move across the floor to Mike, Gez and Tony …

"Ah, here's Chris … followed by Jane and Lucy" advises Tony (Smiling)

"Evening Chris … evening girls" quips Mike (Smiling)

"Hi Mike" replies Jane (Beaming)

"Well hello, Gez" advises Jane (Sexy Smile and Wink)

"Hello, Jane … you look stunning tonight" replies Gez (Winking)

"Well, it's Christmas, darling … I thought I'd give you all a thrill" advises Jane (All Laughing)

Ernest walks over to the bar with Chris and Tony. Mike moves over to speak to Jane and Lucy …

"We've got a job for you both, later" advises Mike (Laughing)

"Well, don't keep us in suspense, what is it?" asks Lucy (Looks puzzled)

"OK … come and have a chat with me and Gez" replies Mike (Motions)

"Well, what have you both got us for

Christmas?" asks Jane
"We'll chat about that later, love" replies Mike/Gez (Nudge/Wink)
"What's going on?" asks Jane (Looks puzzled)
"We're going to spring a surprise on Ernest, tonight" advises Mike (Smiling)

"Yea, for services rendered … and David will be here tonight to present the prize" advises Gez (Laughing)
"OK … what do you want us both to do, darling?" asks Jane/Lucy (Smiling)
"When we spring the surprise … both of you on Ernest's arm" replies Mike (Laughing)
"He'll love that" advises Gez (Laughing)

"OK … we'll do it on one condition" reply Jane/Lucy (Smiling)

"Name it?" replies Mike (Looks intrigued)
"You both look after us, afterwards" replies Jane (Smiling)
"OK … it's a done deal" advises Mike (Laughing)
"Second that" responds Gez (All Smiling)

"OK, keep it all under wraps for now" advises Mike

"We'll be making an announcement shortly … and there's a buffet and a Christmas disco" explains Mike
"Yea … the only way is up for you two girls" replies Gez (Laughing)

The DJ starts up the disco by playing lots of Christmas hits …

Everyone piles on to the dance floor …

"Come on Gez … time for a Christmas dance with me and Lucy" advises Jane (Pulls Gez on to the floor)

"Wait for me" replies Mike (Laughing)
After several dances, Mike and Gez retreat from the dance floor …

David … The Zodiac Regional Manager, arrives at Tapas, from his office in Leeds City Centre …
"Welcome, David" greets Mike (Smiling/Shaking Hands)

"Hello Mike … is everything in place for our surprise guest?" asks David

"Yea … and we've lined up two lovely girls to accompany him" explains Mike
"Yes … Jane and Lucy have agreed to be Ernest's escorts when we spring the surprise" advises Gez (Smiles)
"Do you think he suspects?" asks David (Smiling)

"I doubt it … Ernest's a bit of a Jack the Lad … he loves his ladies" quips Mike

"OK … we'll do it in about half an hour … approx 9.30pm … the bar should be quite full by then" explains David
"Yes … that's fine with us" reply Mike/Gez (All Laughing)

It's fast approaching 9.30pm … time for David to work his magic … The DJ stops all dancing ... David takes to the floor ...

"If you could all please gather round ... I have several announcements to make" advises David (Smiling)

"Yea ... quiet please ... that means you Chris, at the back ... and Tony put that lady down" reply Mike/Gez (Everyone Laughing)

"It's not only a special time at Christmas" advises David

"Tonight, we're here to thank a very special member" explains David

"There is one among us, who is a reluctant hero ... one who put his life on the line for his country ... and I know he doesn't want anyone to know it ... but he was a distinguished Warrant Officer and took part in the infamous Dam Buster's raid" explains David (Smiling)

"Oh no ... what have you done?" asks Ernest (Looks embarrassed)

"Ernest it's OK ... please come forward" asks David (Lots of applause from Zodiac members)

"OK, Jane and Lucy ... if you could take up your positions?" asks Mike

"Mike, what are you saying?" replies Jane (Everyone Laughing)

Ernest steps forward and is greeted with very loud cheers ...

"Ernest ... on behalf of Zodiac, Leeds ... I'd like to present you with a Gold Card ... there's only 6 in the country, and you have one" advises David (More

applause)
"We'd also like to give you this bottle of champagne and vouchers for you and a lady of your choice for a meal at any restaurant in Leeds" explains David (Loud applause)
Jane and Lucy enter the dance floor …

"We're part of the package … we're your escorts tonight" advise Jane/Lucy

"Does that mean …" asks Ernest (Laughing)
"No, it bloody well doesn't, Ernest" replies Jane (Everyone Laughing)

"Well, Ernest … would you like to say anything to your adoring fans?" asks David (Clapping)

"Thank you, David … yes I would" replies Ernest (Smiles)
"Thank you to Mike and Gez and all our members … you just don't know how much this means to me" advises Ernest (Still smiling)
"I'm so glad that I joined Zodiac and all the friends I have made. It was an honour to serve my Country … and it's an honour to be with you all tonight, and I hope to be for a long time to come" explains Ernest (With a tear in his eye)
"Thanks Ernest, your a kind of hero here now" replies David
"Your also a Gold Card holder … even I don't have one of those" explains David (All Laughing)
"Yep … your number one here now"
advises Gez (Laughing)

"Top man" replies Mike (Laughing)
Stella, a stunning blonde in her late forties, steps forward ...

"I'd like you to come to my party, Ernest on New Year's Eve ... will you come?" asks Stella (Smiling)
"Yes, of course ... I'll wear my kilt"
quips Ernest (Laughing)
"We have got to leave you now" advise
Jane/Lucy
"Ernest, come and join us on the dance floor" advise Mike/Gez (Motions)
The DJ starts up and plays SIMPLY THE BEST ... it's the Zodiac anthem ... Everyone piles on to the dance floor ...
"All on the dance floor ... they are playing my song" advises Ernest (Laughing)

Mike suddenly has a brilliant idea ...

"What do you think about a Christmas Limbo Contest?" asks Mike (Laughing)

"Good idea" replies Gez (Laughing)
"I'll announce it ... Ernest you can be the judge" advises Mike (Laughing)
"What an honour" replies Ernest (Laughing)
The DJ temporarily stops the next
record from playing ...
"Is this microphone on?" asks Mike
"Oh, yea ... it's on" explains Mike (All Laughing)

"OK, in honour of Ernest's special night we are going to have a Christmas Limbo Contest" advises Mike

(Laughing)
"How low can you go" replies Gez (Laughing)
"Right, when our DJ, Andy, plays the next reggae song that's when we'll do Limbo" explains Mike (Pointing)
"Ladies, please look after your modesty when under the pole" advises Mike (Laughing)
"Oh, spoilsport … I was looking forward to that" replies Ernest (More Laughing)
"We don't want you to go all loopy on us, Ernest" advises Gez (Laughing)
"No chance of that, lad" responds Ernest (Everyone Laughing)

It's Limbo time … Mike and Gez are the pole holders … and as promised, Ernest is the judge …
"Hang on Mike … what's the prize for the winner?" asks Stella (Smiling)

"A night out with me, love … and a nice meal in Leeds" quips Ernest (Laughing)

"Hang on, what if a fella wins?" asks Stella (Laughing)
"Then, it'll be two nights out with me" advises Ernest (All Laughing)
"Seriously Ernest … we are making it an all ladies contest, in your honour" explains Mike (All Laughing)
"OK, let's get this show on the road" quips Ernest (Laughing)
The DJ sets the music and Ernest takes his chair as the judge … Mike and

Gez are in position with the pole and microphones …
"Steady the pole lad … we're both shaking a bit" advises Mike (Laughing)
"OK, we're cool … and ready for you girls to go" replies Gez (Laughing)
First up … Jane

"Wow up and under … you're a professional … nice legs love" quips Mike

"How did I do, Ernest?" asks Jane
"Got my pecker up, love" quips Ernest (All Laughing)
Second up … Lucy

"Don't look at my knickers, Ernest" advises Lucy (All Laughing)
"I'll try my best to, love" replies Ernest (More Laughing)
"Ernest is in his element" advises Mike (Laughing)
He's really enjoying himself, Mike" replies Gez (Laughing)

Next up, Stella …

"I hope you like my dance, Ernest?" asks Stella

"I'm sure I will, love" replies Ernest (Laughing)
Mike turns to Gez and moves the pole even lower …
"You know what … this could go on all night" quips Mike
"Tell you what, let's cut it short, Mike" replies Gez (Laughing)
"Why, Gezza?" asks Mike
"I think Ernest's keen on Stella" advises Gez (Laughing)
"What, fix the contest?" asks Mike
"Yea … for Ernest" replies Gez (Laughing)

"OK … let's do it" advises Mike (Both Laughing)

"OK … Mr DJ if you could stop the music" asks Gez
"Yea … Ernest has decided the winner is

… Stella" advises Mike
"Have I?" replies Ernest (Looks stunned)
"Yes … your both well matched" replies Gez (Laughing)
"Hey … we're not on Blind Date are we lad?" asks Ernest (All Laughing)
Mike takes to the microphone to announce …
"OK, everyone … it's time for our Christmas buffet" advises Mike
"Yes … the Christmas disco will continue later" replies Gez (Points to Buffet)
Stella taps Mike on the shoulder …
"Mike … can you please give out my New Year's Eve do?" asks Stella (Smiling)
"Yes, of course, it'll be a pleasure, love" replies Mike (Smiling)
"You are coming, aren't you?" asks Stella (Smiling)
"Yea … we all are, love" adds Mike
Mike switches on the microphone …
"Right, if I could have your attention please … you need to get your New Year's Eve Fancy Dress Party tickets this evening from Stella, if you haven't already got one … bring your own bottle and plate as per usual … tickets two quid" advises Mike (Laughing)
"Yes, a bargain … we'll see you all there" replies Gez (Laughing)

Ernest moves over to speak to Mike and Gez …

"You know, you both made an old man, very happy tonight" advises Ernest (Laughing)
"Your welcome mate, very welcome … it's the least we could do" reply Mike/Gez (Smiling)
"Ernest, as a matter of fact … just how old are you?" asks Gez (Looks serious)
"I'll be 63, next month" replies Ernest (Smiling)
Jane returns and moves over to be with Gez …

"You look so young Ernest … how do you do it?" asks Jane (Smiling)

"Oh, I put it down to the big V … Viagra to you love" replies Ernest (Laughing)

"Well, you did ask" quips Ernest (Smiling)
"Yea, she did …didn't she" replies Mike (Laughing)

"There's life in the old dog yet, Ernest" quips Gez (All Laughing)

NEW YEAR'S EVE BASH

It's now New Year's Eve … Zodiac members are gathering at a house in Moortown, near Leeds. Everyone is in fancy dress and quite sozzled!
Inside of Stella's detached house … 9pm … three hours before the Midnight celebrations …
Gez arrives at Stella's house and is greeted by the host …

"Hi … thanks for coming to my party, Gez" greets Stella (Kiss on cheek)

"I like your outfit, love … nicely put together" replies Gez (Laughing)

"Your looking quite sexy too" replies Stella (Big Smile)
"I like your 1920's gear and your hat, very roaring twenties" replies Stella
"Oh, I've come as Elliot Ness" quips Gez (Laughing)
"The Untouchables?" replies Stella (Sexy smile)

"Yes, that's it Stella … but I'm very touchable tonight" advises Gez (Laughing)

"Cheeky" responds Stella (Winking)
"I bet you say that to all the girls?" replies Stella (Laughing)
"Any road, you look like a bit of a raver?" advises Gez (Smiling)

Stella is dressed in a Sixties pink and black mini dress with matching hat and way out gear …
"Oh, I'm a girl from the Swinging Sixties" advises Stella (Beaming smile)
"Well, you look really sexy in your mini dress, love" replies Gez (Looks impressed)
Mike enters the party …

"Yea, she looks a bit of alright, doesn't she" adds Mike (Laughing)

Mike is dressed as Bertie Basset and looks a proper nana …

Mike's fancy dress costume is made up of various liquorice allsorts

"Like the outfit, Mike" quips Gez (Lauging)
"Thought it might attract some attention" advises Mike (All Laughing)
"Well, it certainly has" replies Stella (Smiling)
"Yea, Bertie Basset … your already to eat" quips Gez (Laughing)
"The only problem is … it's getting hot in this suit" adds Mike (All Laughing)

Ernest enters the party, and is met by Stella at the door …

"Your looking a bit flash tonight, Ernest" advises Mike
Ernest is dressed in a flamboyant kilt and really looks the part …
"What the heck are you wearing, Ernest?"

asks Gez (Laughing)
"Oh, I'm a Scotsman … full kilt and all" replies Ernest (Laughing)
"Och aye the noo" replies Mike (All Laughing)

"Well, what are you wearing underneath?" asks Mike (Laughing)

"Yes, come on … don't keep us in suspenders, love" asks Stella (Laughing)

"Why the mighty haggis of course" quips Ernest (Everyone Laughing)

"It's bound to put a smile on any girl's face" adds Ernest (More Laughing)
Tony arrives at Stella's bash … dressed as Flash Gordon …

"You look a bit flash tonight, Tony … get it?" asks Mike (Laughing)

"Gordon's alive" quips Gez (Laughing)
"Oh, yea … thanks pal" replies Tony (Laughing)

"Well, if you think I look like this … what about you two?" adds Tony (Laughing)

"OK, I guess we asked for that, Tony" adds Mike (Laughing)
"Well, you can ring my bell, any day, love" replies Stella (Smiling)

"Ding Dong … I just might tonight, love … I just might" advises Tony (Laughing)

"Tony, you look good mate … you'll certainly get

their attention" quips Gez

"You look good too, Gezza … should be a good night mate" replies Tony (Laughing)

More and more Zodiac members arrive at the New Year's Eve bash ...

Sandra (mid 40s, mousey brown hair, green eyes, attractive) and Jasmine (mid 30s blonde bobbed hair, attractive) ...
"Hi, I'm Sandra ... that's Jasmine ... we're from Leeds" advises Sandra (Smiling)
"Oh, we like your nurse's outfits, love" replies Gez (Laughing)
"Couldn't you get your skirts any shorter, love?" asks Mike (Laughing)

"Well, any shorter ... and we'll be able to see what they had for breakfast" quips Ernest (All Laughing)
"Cheeky ... I like your kilt"
advises Jasmine (Smiling)
"Me, too" adds Sandra (Big Smile)
The music is turned up loud, everyone is on the dance floor ...
"Fancy dancing with an old Scottish soldier?" asks Ernest (Smiling)
"What are you wearing underneath your kilt?" asks Jasmine (Laughing)
"A little of what you fancy, love" quips Ernest (All Laughing)
"Lead on, my good man, lead on" advise Sandra/Jasmine
"Looks like Ernest has pulled ... again" advises Gez (Laughing)
"Oh, he's a fast worker ... and two crackers too" replies Mike (Laughing)

More Ladies arrive at the party …
Bernie (mid 40s, long dark hair, attractive) and Erica (mid 40s, blue eyed blonde, attractive) …
"We thought it was Vicars and Tarts" advises Bernie (Sexy Smile)
"Oh, we like tarts, love" advises Tony (Laughing)
"You both look tarty tonight, love" quips Mike (Laughing)
"What's your names?" asks Tony (Smiling)
"I'm Bernie … this is Erica" advises Bernie (Big Smile)
"Care for a dance, love?" asks Mike (Smiling)
"You can be our pimps" quips Erica (Laughing)
"What an honour" replies Mike (All Laughing)
Suddenly the music changes to … SIMPLY THE BEST by TINA TURNER …
"Right, all on the floor for this" advises Mike (Laughing)
"They all seem to respond to you … are you a manager?" asks Bernie
"No, I run the Leeds bar night with Gez … are you both new?" asks Mike
"Yes, it's our first night, honey" replies Bernie
"Will you look after us?" asks Erica (Big Smile)

"Oh, you can count on it, love" answers Mike (Both Laughing)

IT'S A KIND OF LOVE

"Hi, I'm Gez ... I see you've already met Mike" quips Gez (Laughing)

"Oh ... he's lovely" replies Bernie (Smiling)
"Hello Gez ... I'm Bernie ... this is Erica" replies Bernie (Big Smile)

"Right Gezza ... don't do the short skirts joke ... it's already been done" advises Mike (Laughing)
"We loved Mike's response" reply Bernie/Erica (Smiling)
"He's a real charmer is Mike" replies Gez (Laughing)
"Oh, he is ... he is" quips Gez (Smiling)
"Come to our bar night in Leeds next Tuesday at Tapas ... you'll enjoy meeting people and seeing what's coming up on the Events board" explains Gez (Smiling)
"What about tonight, love?" asks Bernie (Smiling)
"Yea, what about tonight?" replies Erica (Also Smiling)
"Stick around girls ... you never know your luck" quips Mike (Laughing)
"We're looking to get pulled" advises Bernie (Laughing)
"Well, your both really two crackers" advises Mike (Laughing)
"Shag well by name ... shag very well by nature" replies Bernie (All Laughing)
"Is that a joke?" asks Gez (Looks puzzled)
"Wow ... your both fast workers, love" adds Tony

(Laughing)

"When the clock strikes 12 … you'll both get your tickets stamped, good and proper" replies Mike (All Laughing)
Jane and Lucy arrive at the New Year's Eve bash …

They are both dressed as 60s Go Go dancers … and move over to be with Mike and Gez …
"Have you been waiting for me, darling?"
asks Jane (Looks Sexy)
"Who else?" replies Gez (Smiling)
"Do you like my outfit, honey?" asks Jane (Very sexy)

"Oh … it's nice and short and tight in the right places" replies Gez (Laughing)

"If anyone asks what we do …" advises Jane
"We're going to tell them … we shake" replies Jane (All Laughing)
"Shake?" reply Mike/Gez (Laughing)
"Yea … we're both Go Go dancers" explains Jane (All Laughing)

"Well, you've got me going already" replies Mike (Everyone Laughing)

"Yea … and me too" advises Gez (All Laughing)

"You … both hot under the collar for us?" asks Lucy (Laughing)

"Too right, love … you and your 60s outfits" advises Mike (Laughing)

"What about you, darling? asks Jane (Sexy

Wink)

"I'm always hot for you, Jane?" replies Gez (Laughing)

"Gez, is a bit of a dark horse" advises Jane

"Am I?" asks Gez (Looks sheepish)

"Yea, Jane's right Gezza … you play your cards close to your chest" replies Mike

"Yea, you can be sometimes a bit secretive?" explains Mike
"Well I suppose we all have secrets" advises Lucy
"OK, Gezza … now are you going to make my night or what?" asks Jane (All Laughing)
"What?" replies Gez (All Laughing)

"You know what I mean" explains Jane (Smiling)

"Yea, I think I do" replies Gez (Laughing)
"Well, what are you going to do, darling?" asks Jane (Winking)
"OK, Jane … maybe it's time" replies Gez (Smiling)
"I think it's time for a drink, honey" explains Jane (Smiling)
"Yea, OK … Mike, fancy coming for a drink with us?" asks Gez (Points to Bar area)
"It's just you and me, love" explains Jane (Big Smile)
"OK, just you and me" replies Gez (Laughing)

Ernest, arrives on the scene with Jasmine and Sandra …

"Hi, Jane … is he looking after you tonight?" asks Ernest (Smiling)

"Hello, Ernest (Kiss on cheek) … he is love … he's only got eyes for me" advises Jane (Laughing)
"You look to be having a good time,

Ernest?" asks Gez
"Oh, he's a real gentleman, love" replies Jasmine (Smiling)
"Yes, he's of the old school" advises Sandra (Laughing)
"Well, lad … I'd like to talk, but duty calls … come on girls it's time for another dance" replies Ernest (Motions to dance floor)
Stella enters and asks for everyone's attention …

"OK, if I can have your attention, please … just for a minute" explains Stella

"Yes, can we have order, for our lovely hostess" replies Mike (All Laughing)
"We'll be having the buffet in about half an hour … please don't all rush at once" explains Stella (Laughing)
"Did you all remember to bring your own bottle and plate, tonight?" asks Mike
"We'll be having the countdown to Midnight with Big Ben's bongs followed by …" advises Stella (Smiling)
"Lot's of snogging" advises Ernest (All Laughing)

"No groping allowed" explains Mike (More Laughing)

"Spoilsport" replies Ernest (Laughing)
"Except for Ernest … well he is a Gold Card member" advises Mike (Laughing)
"Like being royalty" replies Ernest (All Laughing)
"OK, it's New Year … do as you please"

explains Mike (More Laughing)
"That means you too, darling" advises Jane (Points to Gez and Winks)
"Where was I?" asks Stella (All Laughing)
"Oh, yes ... followed by a toast of bubbly to ... 1989" explains Stella
"OK, it's time for the buffet" advises Mike
Enter Rick from Huddersfield ... followed by Chris ...

"They can get the party started, now I'm here" advises Rick

Rick is in his late forties, short and balding ...
"Who let prick ... into the party?" asks Mike (Laughing)
"Steady on Mike, let it go" advises Gez
"OK, but I don't like it" explains Mike (Looking daggers at Rick)

Chris walks over to talk to Mike and Gez ...

"Hello, Chris ... so glad you could make it, mate" greets Gez (Shaking hands)

"Hi Gez ... sorry I had to follow prick ... I mean, Rick" replies Chris (All Laughing)

"It's OK, Chris ... it's not your fault, prick by name, prick by nature" replies Mike
"Nice outfit, Jane" advises Chris (Smiles)

"Well, thank you, kind, Sir" replies Jane (Beaming)

Stella announces that it is fast approaching Midnight ...

"OK, everyone … we're close to Midnight … everyone on the dance floor" advises Stella (Motions)

Mike turns up the volume on the radio … "OK, everyone … here we go" advises Mike
"Countdown … 5 4 3 2 1 Big Ben's Bongs … Happy New Year" shouts Mike
"OK … take your partners … time to seal it with a kiss" advises Stella
"OK, Jane, give us a kiss … another New Year with you" advises Gez (Snogging)
"And with you, darling" replies Jane (More Snogging)
"Happy New Year, Mike and Tony"
shouts Gez (Laughing)
"Same to you, mate" replies Mike/Tony
(Both Laughing)
"How are you getting on, Ernest?" asks
Gez
"Oh, my pecker is in it's element, with two lovely girls" advises Ernest (Laughing)
"Ernest's jolly pecker … is at it again" advises Mike (Everyone Laughing)
"What about my kiss, Gez?" asks Jean

"Well, what are we waiting for?" replies Gez (Snogging)

Jean, mid forties, short blonde hair, attractive …

"We'll have to have a night out, sometime"
asks Jean (Winking)

"Yea, maybe we will, sometime" replies Gez

"OK, it's time for bubbly" advises Stella (Big Smile)

"Oh, bubbly always goes to my head" replies Jasmine (Laughing)

"Me, too … one drink, and I'm anybodies" advises Sandra (All Laughing)

"Don't worry, I'll look after you both" advises Ernest (Laughing)

"… and we promise to look after you, Ernest" advises Sandra (Big Smile)
"OK, it's time to party until the small hours" announces Stella
Mike starts to look for Gez …

"Where's Gezza … anyone seen Gezza?" asks Mike (Looks concerned)

"He's a bit groggy … gone outside for a breather" advises Jane
"I'll go and see if he's OK" replies Mike (Looks concerned)
"Yea, I'll come too" advises Chris
"Me, too" replies Tony (Follows Mike)

Gez is wandering about the garden …

"Are you OK, Gezza?" asks Mike (Looks concerned)

"Yea, I'm OK, Mike … everything went a bit dizzy in there" replies Gez

"We've two nurses on call … in very short skirts … can they help?" asks Mike (All Laughing)
"I'm sure they can" advises Gez (More Laughing)

"I've never asked you … but just how old are you?" asks Mike

"I'm 35, and it's my birthday … well it was on New Year's Eve" explains Gez

Jane enters, looking very concerned …
"Is my Gez, OK?" asks Jane

"He's looking for a kind nurse, love"
replies Mike (Laughing)

"Well, he's got one here" advises Jane (Smiling)
"Now is there anything I can do for you, darling?" asks Jane (Big Smile)
"Yea … Gezza needs some TLC" advises Tony (Everyone Laughing)
"We all do really, love" adds Mike (More Laughing)

Rick enters the scene …

"What's up with him?" asks Rick
"They'll be something up with you … if you don't belt up" replies Mike (Looks serious)
"It's OK, Mike … I'm alright" advises Gez
"I suppose he can't take his booze" replies Rick

"Right, that's quite enough" answers Mike (Looks miffed)

Rick squares up to Mike …

"Mike/Rick … I want you to shake hands … this is a New Year … let's start it off right" adds Gez
"Well?" asks Mike (Still mad)

"Well … OK by me"
replies Rick

"Yea … alright
then" advises Mike
(Reluctant)

Both men shake hands
…

"What are we all doing here out here?" asks Tony

"There's a party going on in there … let's carry on" advises Chris

Stella arrives on the scene …

"Is Gez, OK, Jane?" asks Stella (Looking very concerned)

"Yes, he's fine love … I'll look after him" advises Jane (Smiling)

Gez turns to Jane …

"Give me another kiss, Jane" asks Gez

"Is Gez, alright, Jane?" asks Lucy

"Yes … I have him under my spell" replies Jane

"Here's to all that 1989 will bring" replies Gez (All Laughing)

CHRISTMAS IN JULY/ SUMMER BAR BQ

Moving on into 1989, and it's another action packed time at Zodiac. It is also the dawn of a new era with changes taking place in 1990 in a very big way ... Mike and Gez in conversation at Tapas ...

"So, are you going to the party, Mike?" asks Gez

"Yea ... I've got my ticket, have you?" replies Mike

"Oh, yea ... weeks ago" advises Gez

"I'm thinking of having a Summer Bar BQ at my place ... are you up for it?" asks Mike (Laughing)

"Yes, of course ... count me in" replies Gez (Smiling)

"We'll set up all the arrangements after this weekend's party" advises Mike (Looks enthusiastic)

"OK, I'll get some tapes ready for dancing" replies Gez (Smiles)

Everyone is talking about the weekend of the CHRISTMAS IN JULY party in Harrogate ... Zodiac members are advised to WEAR SOMETHING IN RED ... Ernest arrives at Tapas, and obviously gives his take on the up coming event ...

"What have you got for the do at the weekend,

Ernest?" asks Mike (Looks serious)
"Red tie, red shirt?" asks
Gez (Laughing)
"It's a surprise" quips
Ernest (Winking)
"OK ... I think I'll go for the red tie this time ... it's an easy option" advises Mike (Smiling)
Tony arrives at Tapas and meanders across to Mike and company ...
"Are you going to the party, Tony?" asks
Gez (Smiles)
"We're both going" advises Mike (Smiling)
"Yea ... I've got my ticket ... see you all at the party" adds Tony
It's the weekend of the Christmas in July Party in Harrogate ...
Gez arrives at the address, and is met by the host ...

"Hi ... I'm Melanie ... thank you for coming to my party" advises Melanie

"Call me Mel" explains Melanie (Lovely smile)
Mel is a brunette, in her mid forties, attractive ...
"OK ... you can call me Gez" replies Gez (Smiling)
"Tony and Mike from Leeds are already here" advises Mel (Points to Lounge)
"My partners in crime" explains Gez (Laughing)
"We've lots of people coming tonight ... so

mingle" replies Mel (Smiling)
Gez joins Mike and Tony, and they meander over to the drinks section …
Suddenly, Mike becomes agitated …
"Oh, look out"
advises Mike
"Why?" asks Gez
"Prick has just arrived" explains Mike (All Laughing)

"Who?" asks Mel (Looks surprised)

"Oh, Rick to you and me … but otherwise known as …" advises Mike (Laughing)
"Ah, yes … now I get it" adds
Mel (Also Laughing)
"Have you been up to anything,
Tony?" asks Gez
"Checking out everything"
replies Tony (Smiling)
Ernest arrives at the party … and takes everyone by surprise …

"Good evening, gentlemen … it's going to be a good night" proclaims Ernest (Laughing)
"Do you like my Christmas gear?" asks
Ernest (Still Laughing)
"Woah … you look a proper Charley" advises Mike (All Laughing)
"Well, I did tell you it was a surprise" adds
Ernest (Laughing)
"Your not kidding, mate" replies Tony (All Laughing)
Ernest is dressed in the full Santa outfit complete

with white beard ... and it's July ...
"You must be as hot as hell in that outfit" explains Mike (All Laughing)

"I am, but I'm hoping to sit a few girls on my lap" replies Ernest (Smiling)

"OK, point me in the right direction" adds Ernest (Laughing)
"Food and drink over there ... all the ladies that away" replies Mike (Laughing)
"Ernest's in his element" adds Gez (Laughing)
The party music starts up and various hit songs are being played ...
"They are playing my song" shouts Ernest
The full Christmas mix of hits are now playing ...

"It feels weird celebrating Christmas in July" advises Gez (Laughing)

"Yea ... but that's when they do it down under" explains Mike
"It's for real there ... they have their winter in July" adds Tony
"Weird" adds Mike (Laughing)
"Still any excuse ... for a party" advises Mike

Jane and Lucy from York arrive in the skimpiest of Santa outfits ...

"Wow ... look at you two" advises Mike (Smiling)
"Full on costumes tonight" adds Tony
"... and so little of it" replies Gez (Smiling)

Jane moves across to Gez …

"Well, darling … what do you think?" asks Jane (Big Smile)

"Do you like me in this, honey?" adds Jane

"In and out of it, Jane" advises Gez (Big Smile)

"Oh, you've got a lovely body" replies Ernest (Smiling)

"Well, there's nothing wrong with his eyesight" adds Mike (All Laughing)

Suddenly, the Zodiac anthem starts to play … SIMPLY THE BEST by TINA TURNER …

"Well, are we dancing or what?" asks Jane (Big Smile)

"Well, yea … but I don't know where to put my hands" replies Gez (Smiling)

"All over me, darling … all over me" responds Jane (Big Smile)

"Maybe … but not here" adds Gez (Looks embarrassed)

"Later then, honey" adds Jane (Smiling)

"By the way … put your eyeballs back in their sockets" advises Jane (All Laughing)

"You really look stunning tonight, Jane" advises Gez (Smiling)

"Lucy, you look fab too" adds Gez (Blows a kiss)

"Thanks, darling" replies Lucy (Big Smile)

"Now you've got us both" advises
Jane (Smiling)

"You've got our full attention"
adds Lucy (Smiling)
"Well, what are you going to do … double trouble?"
explains Jane (Smiling)

The following Saturday, Mike's Summer Bar BQ is on at his house in Morley. Tickets are selling fast at the Bar Night in Tapas …
Gez arrives at Tapas and is met by Mike …

"How's the tickets going for the Bar BQ, Mike?" asks Gez

"I've sold over 70 tickets already" advises
Mike (Looks stunned)

"Well, your a popular man here, mate"
replies Gez (Smiling)

"Can you take the numbers at your place?" asks Gez (Looks concerned)
"Oh, yea … I think we'll go for the ton"
replies Mike (Laughing)
"What do you think of Sam?" asks Mike
"Who?" replies Gez (Looks surprised)
"Oh, she's just joined … we're already getting on like a house on fire" adds Mike (Laughing)
Sam greets Gez and she certainly is a
very refined lady …
"Hi, I'm Sam" greets a voice
Sam is a lovely blonde, slim and very attractive …

"Hi, I'm Gez … I suppose Mike has told you everything about me?" asks Gez

"Well, not everything obviously" adds Mike
"You see, my mate Gez is different to others here" explains Mike
"In what way, love?" asks Sam
"He's very protective … we think he's hiding a secret" advises Mike
"Secret … what secret?" asks Gez (Looks stunned)
"I don't know … but your hiding something" explains Mike
Sam goes off to powder her nose …
"Your in there, mate" advises Gez (Laughing)

"Is Sam coming to your Bar BQ at the weekend?" asks Gez (Smiling)

"Yea, what do you think" replies Mike (Smiling)
"Your a fast worker, Mike" adds Gez (Laughing)

Gez advises Mike that he has an idea for the weekend …

"I've been thinking, Mike … I've got an idea" adds Gez (Smiling)

"What is it, mate?" asks Mike (Smiling)
"Remember the limbo contest we did for Ernest?" asks Gez
"Yea, I remember, that made it a good night" replies Mike
"Well, what if we do it again at your

Bar BQ?" asks Gez
"Oh, yea ... how low can you go?" adds Mike (Laughing)
"Good idea, Gezza" advises Mike (All Laughing)
"I think all the Zodiac members will love it" advises Gez (Laughing)
"Limbo dancing with a difference" explains Gez (Laughing)
"How low can you go under the bar to the music" adds Mike (Laughing)
"OK, I'm up for that, we'll do it on Saturday" explains Mike
"Is Ernest coming, Mike?" asks Gez

"Oh, he was the first to buy a ticket" adds Mike (Smiling)

"Jane and Lucy are coming too" advises Mike (Laughing)
"Don't worry ... there will be lots of other girls too" explains Mike (All Laughing)
"If I know you ... there will be more girls than fellas" replies Gez (Laughing)
"Gezza ... you know me too well" responds Mike (All Laughing)
"No prick ... I mean Rick ... all tickets are sold, if he asks" explains Mike (Laughing)
"I agree" adds Gez (Laughing)

The weekend of Mike's Summer Bar BQ arrives ... Somewhere in Morley, on the outskirts of Leeds

...

Mike and Gez are busy preparing the evening for the Bar BQ prior to arrival of Zodiac members ...
"Snap" advises Mike

"We're both wearing Hawaiian shirts" explains Mike (Laughing)

"Yea, but mines a bit different to yours" replies Gez (Laughing)

"We'll definitely pull tonight, Gezza" advises Mike
"How do you want us to play it, Mike?" asks Gez (Smiling)

"Just play it casual ... that's all you have to do ... body language will do the rest" explains Mike (Laughing)
"Any road ... tell me more about you ... I know you and yet I don't know you" replies Mike (Smiling)
"Well, there's nothing to tell, really, Mike" advises Gez (Looks coy)
"Nothing to tell?" adds Mike (Looks stunned)
"What do you mean, mate?" replies Mike (Looking puzzled)
"Everyone has a past ... mines well worn" explains Mike (Laughing)
"So what about you?" asks Mike
"Perhaps I'll tell you about it one day ... my life has been complicated" replies Gez (Looks embarrassed)
"Complicated in what way, Gezza?" asks Mike (Smiling)

"So you are hiding a secret, then?" adds Mike

(StillLooking puzzled)

Suddenly, Tony and Ernest arrive at Mike's Bar BQ …

"Saved by the bell" replies Gez (Looking relieved)
Tony and Ernest are welcomed by Mike and led into the garden area where the Bar BQ is taking place near the Pagoda …
"So, what have you two been up to?" asks Mike

"I had a superb time last Saturday" replies Ernest (Smiling)

"Except" explains Ernest
"Go on" advises Mike (Looks puzzled)

"That Rick, tried to steal my woman" explains Ernest (Looks mad)

"Did he now?" replies Gez (Looks puzzled)
"I told him where to go … politely of course" adds Ernest (Laughing)
"Rick by name … prick by nature" replies Mike (All Laughing)
"I can't stand that man … there's something about him" advises Tony
"He's a real dick" adds Mike (All Laughing)
"OK we get the picture, Ernest" replies Gez

"Give him enough rope, and he'll hang himself one day" replies Mike (Laughing)

More arrivals enter Mike's garden and come over to the Bar BQ area …
Jane and Lucy also arrive on the scene …

"Nice to see you girls again" advises Mike (Smiling)

Various songs are belting out in the background …

"Well, are you going to give it up to me, tonight?" asks Jane (Smiling)

"It depends" replies Gez (Smiling)
"On what?" asks Jane (Looking stunning)

"On whether you can keep a secret" advises Gez (Smiling)

"See, I knew you were keeping some sort of secret" adds Mike
"No need to keep any secrets, everyone knows I fancy you" replies Jane (Smiling)
"I'm really flattered, Jane" explains Gez (Smiling)

Mike and Lucy come over to Jane …

"Are you going to take part in the Limbo dancing contest?" asks Mike

"What, in this short dress?" replies Jane (Smiling)
"Well, we did tell everyone it was part of the evening, Jane" adds Mike
"OK, maybe … if Lucy does it too?" replies Jane
"What's that?" asks Lucy (Smiling)

"We've been asked to take part in the Limbo dancing, by Mike" adds Jane

"I'll do it … if you do, Jane" explains Lucy
"OK … what have we got to lose?" replies Jane (Smiling)
"Your modesty" replies Ernest (Laughing)
Gez starts up the tape deck and Mike gets into position with the pole …
"Are we all set, Gezza?" asks Mike

"Yea, ready when you are, Mike" replies Gez (Laughing)

Mike takes to the microphone …

"OK … it's time for our Limbo Contest" explains Mike (Smiling)

"How low can you go" replies Gez (Laughing)
"Ladies, keep your hands on your modesty … if you know what I mean?" explains Mike (All Laughing)
"Spoil sport" replies Ernest (Laughing)

"Let's get this show on the road" adds Mike (Smiling)

Gez sets the tape in motion and various reggae tunes are now being played …

"OK, Mike?" asks Gez
"Go for it, Gezza" replies Mike (Laughing)

Mike barks out the rules of the Limbo Contest …

"Right … the one that can go the lowest, gets a special prize" advises Mike

"What is it?" asks Jane

"A night out with me" explains Mike (All Laughing)

"No, you'll get a bottle of bubbly … and then a night out with me" adds Mike (Everyone Laughing)
"Or with Ernest … if you wish" advises Gez (Laughing)
"OK, who's first?" asks Mike
"OK, I'll do it" advises Ernest (Laughing)

"Are you sure … remember your dodgy back" advises Mike (Smiling)

"OK, go on, Ernest" advises Gez
"Up and under … nice one, Ernest" adds Mike (Laughing)
"OK, you now, Jane" replies Gez (Smiling)
Jane manoeuvres the pole and keeps her modesty in tact …

"Nice one, love … kept your hand as instructed" explains Mike (Smiling)

"Oh, I wanted to see next weeks washing" shouts Ernest (All Laughing)

"Has he no shame?" asks Jane (Looks mad)
"No" replies Ernest (Smiling)

The Limbo Contest suddenly comes to an end, and the tapes are changed to smooch music …
Jane turns to Gez …

"Well, are you going to smooch with me, darling?" asks Jane (Smiling)

"OK, sure, Janie" replies Gez (Smiling)

"Don't call me Janie, love … it sounds so common" advises Jane (Smiling)
"Do you remember the Jane cartoon in the newspapers?" adds Jane
"Oh, it was a kind of caricature/cartoon … she was always showing her knickers and suspenders" replies Gez (Laughing)
"I remember too" adds Mike
(Laughing)
"Down boy" replies Jane
(Smiling)
The next Bar night at Tapas and Mike's Bar BQ is the talking point of the evening …

Tony enters Tapas and connects with Mike in the Bar area …

"It was a fab Bar BQ on Saturday, Mike" advises Tony (Smiling)
"Thanks, I'm glad you enjoyed yourself, Tony" replies Mike (Laughing)
"How did you make out with Sam?" asks Gez (Smiling)
"Oh, perfect … a very nice fit" adds Mike (Laughing)

"I think we get the picture, Mike" explains Gez (Laughing)

"What about you with Jane?" asks Mike
"Your in there" explains
Tony (Laughing)
"Well in" adds Mike
(Laughing)

"What's up next?" asks Tony

"I'm going to check out the events board" advises Tony (Smiling)

"OK, Gezza what's going on with you and Jane?" asks Mike (Smiling)

"We're just good friends, that's all, Mike" responds Gez (Laughing)

"Your on the defensive again" explains Mike
"Remember the saying … don't wash your dirty laundry in public?" replies Gez
"Well, I'm keeping it under my hat" explains Gez (Laughing)
"I agree, and very wise too, I'm proud of you, mate" replies Mike (Laughing)

Tony returns, and advises about an upcoming event …

"Well, Tony, have you seen anything that takes your fancy?" asks Mike

"There's a 60s/70s party at Normanton this weekend" advises Tony

"Sounds like fun" replies Mike (Smiling)
"Are we all going?" asks Gez

"You betcha … I mean is the Pope Catholic?" adds Mike (Smiling)

"Well, the event is being staged at the Parish Hall of St John the Baptist" replies Tony
"Hey, I'm Catholic … no need to take the Michael" explains Gez (Looks serious)

"Gez this is Sam" advises Mike (Smiling)
"Hi Sam ... I hope Mike is looking after you" replies Gez (Smiling)

Sam is in her late forties, light brown hair, blue eyes ...

"Yes, he is love ... he's a real charmer" replies Sam
"See what I mean ... it works every time" advises Mike (Laughing)
"Listen and learn" explains Mike
"Oh, I will, Mike, I will" replies Gez (Laughing)

"We're all going to the do in Normanton at the weekend ... are you coming Sam?" asks Tony (Smiling)
"Oh, try and stop me" replies Sam (Beaming)
"Is it fancy dress?" asks Sam
"No, come as you wish ... Mike usually does" replies Gez (Smiling)
It's the weekend of the 60's/70's party at Normanton ...
Mike, Gez, and Tony arrive in good time. They are greeted by Linda at the entrance of the Hall.
"Hi, I'm Linda ... thanks for coming to my party" advises Linda

Linda is a tall red head, wearing a 60s type dress, has green eyes and quite attractive ...
"Hello I'm Tony ... boys I think I've died and gone to heaven" replies Tony (Laughing)
Linda smiles at Tony's remark ...

"Flattery will get you everywhere, Tony" beams Linda

"Hi Linda ... I'm Mike, this is Gez, you've already met Tony" replies Mike (Smiling)

The DJ starts to get the party going with the Loco motion song ...
Everyone links behind each other as if they are in a train and dance along to the song ...
"Come on, Gezza" shouts Mike (Pointing)

Gez makes his way across the floor but is pulled to one side by the Parish Priest ...

"Hey, don't I know you?" asks the priest
"I don't know, do you?" asks Gez (Looking puzzled)

"I'm sure I've seen you before, somewhere" replies the priest

Gez shrugs his shoulders then continues to take to the dance floor ...

"Come on, Gez" shouts Mike
Everyone in the dance hall takes to the floor, but it is a sublime moment for Gez ...

Has he been recognised? Has someone finally got his attention?

We had another two events to choose from for New Year's Eve this year. One in York or the other in Leeds.
Gez chooses to go to the one in Harrogate Road, Leeds ...

Several hours before Midnight ... the party is in full swing at a private house.

Gez knocks on the door …

"Hi … welcome to my party" greets Sandra (a good looking blonde woman)

"Hello, Sandra … I'm Gez" advises Gez
"Don't I know you from Leeds Bar night at Tapas?" asks Sandra
"Yes, that's right, love … I run it with Mike" explains Gez (Smiling)
"I like your gear" quips Sandra (Smiling)
"Oh, I'm supposed to be a character from a TV series" advises Gez (Laughing)
"Well, it's very authentic, love" laughs Sandra
"Yours is a very curvy outfit, Sandra" replies Gez (Laughing)
"Flattery will get you everywhere, Gez" advises Sandra (Big Smile)
"Are all the gang here?" asks Gez (Smiling)
"Tony is somewhere over there, love" advises Sandra
"Well, I suggest you mingle, Gez … I'll see you later" replies Sandra (Smiling)
Gez moves across to the Bar area where he stashes his non alcoholic beer and plate for the buffet …
Another woman, Nicola, catches his eye and both exchange pleasantries …
"Hi, I'm Nicola" greets a voice (Smiling)
"Hi, Nicola … I'm Gez" advises Gez (Smiling)

"I like your outfit … what have you come as, Nicola?" asks Gez

"Oh … I'm the naughty fairy" replies

Nicola (Laughing)
" … and she is too" replies Tony (Laughing)

Gez and Tony shake each other's hands in greeting …

"Hey up, Tony … how long have you been here?" asks Gez (Laughing)

"Not long mate" replies Tony (Laughing)
"Well, Nicola … you can cast a spell on me" advises Gez (Smiling)

"Oh, I will later, honey … don't worry I'll make all your wishes come true" responds Nicola (Laughing)
"I bet you will, saucy minx" replies Gez (Laughing)

Another girl, Rebecca comes across to talk to Tony and Gez. Rebecca is in her late 30s, has long auburn hair, brown eyes …
"Who have you come as?" asks Tony (Smiling)

"Oh, Felicity Shagwell" replies Rebecca (Laughing)

"Who?" asks Gez
"Really?" replies Tony (Laughing)

"Shag well by name … shag very well by nature" explains Rebecca (Smiling)

Tony and Gez almost choke on their beers with that answer!
Linda changes the taped music to 80s pop …

"Do you want to dance, Rebecca?" asks Gez (Smiling)
"Why not, love" replies Rebecca (Laughing)

Gez looks around the room and notices that Tony is

talking to a slim blonde …

Gez and Rebecca rejoin Tony …

"Tony how are you getting on, mate?" asks Gez (Smiling)

"Oh, like a house on fire … this is Jean" answers Tony (Smiling)

"Hi, Gez … I've seen you at the Leeds Bar night" explains Jean (Smiling)

"Jean is very flirty … get the picture?" asks Tony (Laughing)
Jean and Rebecca re both laughing at Tony's comment …

"We're just going to the bar, girls … back in a jiffy" adds Tony (Smiling)

Tony and Gez get a refill …

"Are you missing, Jane?" asks Tony (Smiles)

"Oh, no … she's a stunner though"
replies Gez (Smiling)

The evening seems to go by fairly quickly …
It's almost Midnight … Linda has already tuned into a radio station for Big Ben's chimes …
The chimes begin …

"Happy New Year, everybody" shouts Linda

There is lots of kissing and hugging between all members …

"Welcome to 1990" advises Linda (All Laughing)

"Fancy a glass of bubbly?" asks Rebecca (Smiling)
"OK, don't mind if I do" advises Gez (Smiling)
"Where's my kiss?" asks Rebecca (Big Smile)
Gez and Tony shake hands …

"Happy New Year, mate" advises Tony (Laughing)

"Same to you, mate" replies Gez (Laughing)
"Hey, I saw you … snogging away" replies Tony (Smiling)

"Well, you've got to enjoy yourself, Tony" explains Gez (Smiling)

"Too true, mate" adds Tony (Laughing)
Little did I know, but 1990 was going to be the start of everything and life was really about to take off!
"Hey Gezza" advises Tony (Laughing)

"Did you see that bloke in the bathroom?" asks Tony (Smiling)

"What bloke?" asks Gez
"Oh, we were all lining up, waiting to go to the loo …" explains Tony
"And?" asks Gez
"He was caught, by one of the girls … weeing in the sink" adds Tony (Laughing)
"What happened, Tony?" asks Gez (Laughing)
"Everyone took the mickey out of him, when he

came out" explains Tony (Laughing)
"Serves him right" adds Gez
(Laughing)
"Whatever next, Tony?"
explains Gez (Laughing)

A NEW FOUND CONFIDENCE

It's the start of 1990, Gez decides to join MIRAGE in Leeds, to run alongside ZODIAC. The reason being that if there was nothing on at ZODIAC he could go to the other!
It was the start of something wonderful!

Gez notices the advertisement for MIRAGE in the Evening Post, and decides to give them a call …
"Mirage … how can I help
you?" greets a voice
"Hi, I'm Gez … I'm thinking of
joining" advises Gez
"Oh, Hi … I'm Janet … it costs £50 a year, but you can pay it over three months if you wish?" replies Janet
"Tell me more?" asks Gez

"OK … we run various events, in and around Leeds. We meet on Thursday evenings at Jacomelli's in Leeds city centre … how does it sound?" asks Janet

"Do you know it?" asks Janet
"No, but I'll find it" adds Gez

"It's very central, opposite the Griffin Hotel" explains Janet

"Oh, great … just great" replies Gez
"OK, come down to our Bar night on Thursday, and we'll discuss more details then" replies Janet
"See you then" replies Gez

"OK, see you then, love"
advises Janet.

The call ends ...
Thursday night arrives, and it's first night nerves, all over again, for Gez ...
Gez enters the swish surroundings on the first floor ...

"Hi, I'm Gez ... I phoned Janet, a few days ago" advises Gez (Smiling)

"That'll be me, love" answers a voice
Janet is in her late forties, has curly brown hair, green eyes, wearing spectacles ...
"Hi Janet, I'm Gez" advises Gez (Smiling)

"Are you from Leeds, Gez?" asks Janet (Big Smile)

"Well, I live on the outskirts ... you won't hold that against me will you" asks Gez (Smiling)
"Of course not, as long as you hold it against me" replies Janet (Laughing)
"That's a joke" adds Janet (Both Laughing)
"Right, you got me with that one, love" answers Gez (Laughing)
"Oh, you were pulling my leg" adds Gez (Laughing)
"Lucky she wasn't pulling your plonker" adds another voice (All Laughing)
"Right love, I take it you want to join, Mirage?" asks Janet
"Yes, I'd love to" explains Gez

"OK, I'll get things running with your membership

"... you go and have a look at our Events board, see what's coming up" advises Janet (Smiling)
"OK, Janet ... don't mind if I do" replies Gez

Gez notices a few events on the horizon and begins to make a note of the date and times ...
Suddenly, another voice greets him ...

"Hi ... I'm Jackie" greets the voice (Big Smile)

Jackie is a curly haired blonde lady, in her forties, nicely dressed and attractive ...

"Hi Jackie... I'm Gez" replies Gez
"Would you like to give a do?" asks Jackie (Smiling)
"A do?" replies Gez (Looking shocked)
"Yea, would you like to run an event for us" adds Jackie (Smiling)

"Well, it's my first night, love ... let me get my feet under the table first, besides I don't know where I would stage it" responds Gez (Smiling)
"You can put it on at The Green Community Centre in Horsforth" replies Jackie
"That's where most of our parties are held ... you can sell your tickets to all our members ... will you do it?" asks Jackie (Big Smile)
"Your very persuasive, Jackie" replies Gez (Smiling)
"Well, will you do it?" asks Jackie
"Go on, you've persuaded me" replies Gez (Looks stunned)

"It'll be a disco" explains Gez (Laughing)

"I'll give you all the information at the next Bar night" adds Gez (Smiling)

Suddenly another voice appears on the scene …

"I see they've persuaded you, then?" asks the voice

"Oh, yea … good and proper, mate" replies Gez

"Hi I'm Danny … it is your first night?" asks the voice (Both shaking hands)

"Hi Danny, I'm Gez … yea it's my first night, but I'm not new to all of this" explains Gez (Smiling)

"Oh?" asks Danny (Looks puzzled)

"I'm a member of Zodiac, too" explains Gez (Laughing)

"I thought if there's nothing on there, I might come here" adds Gez

"Your right … what a good idea" replies Danny (Laughing)

Danny introduces Dave to Gez …

"This is Dave, he does all the music at the Community Centre" advises Danny

"Hi, Gez … well I do it with taped music, actually" advises Dave (Smiling)

"Wow … I'm really impressed, I must see you in action" advises Gez (Looks stunned)

"Oh you will, on Saturday … are you coming to our disco?" asks Dave

"Oh, I wouldn't miss it, we'll all be there" advises Danny

"Yea, but just what have I done?" asks Gez (Looks surprised)

"I saw you talking to Jackie … has she persuaded you to give a do?" asks Dave (Looks concerned)

"Yea … but what am I going to do?" replies Gez

"I have to do it now, I said I would" explains Gez (Looks anxious)

"Don't worry" advises Danny

"We'll help you on the night" explains Dave (Laughing)

It's the beginning of February 1990. Gez decides to hold a "Celebration disco" on Saturday 24th of March.

Gez had no need to worry. It became his first SOLD OUT event, and more followed …

Thursday night, Bar night at Jacomelli's in Leeds …

"Hi, I'm Gez … please buy a ticket for my first event at The Green" asks Gez

Sarah, a tall brunette, wanders over to Gez …

"Can I buy a ticket, love?" asks Sarah (Smiling)

"One for me and my mate, Margaret" explains Sarah

"Yes, of course, love" replies Gez (Laughing)

Gez hands over the tickets … Sarah grabs his hand …

"Make sure you come over to dance with me"

advises Sarah (Big Smile)

"But I'll be running the event, love" explains Gez (Smiling)
"Oh, you can put it on auto pilot, can't you?" replies Sarah (Beaming)
The day of the Celebration disco arrives, and its a sell out …

Early evening at the Green Community Centre in Horsforth …

Gez is busy setting up his make shift music centre with matching speakers …

"Will you dance with me, tonight, Gez?" asks a voice
"Of course I will love" replies Gez (Smiling)

Danny enters the upstairs room and meanders over to Gez …

"Well, you seem to be getting on like a house on fire" advises Danny (Laughing)

"Oh, I am mate" replies Gez (Laughing)
"I do a spot of disco myself … present it I
mean" advises Danny
"Another DJ?" adds Gez (Laughing)
"Oh, yea, and Dave too … well he's
resident" explains Danny
"The three Amigo's" laughs Gez
Gez plays all sorts of disco during the evening …

"It's been a fab night, Gezza" advises Stacey (a petite blue eyed blonde)

"Want to walk me home?" asks Stacey (Smiling)
"Where do you live?" asks
Gez (Smiling)
"On the outskirts of Leeds"
advises Stacey (Big Smile)
"Well, I can drop you off, if you want, love?" replies Gez (Smiling)
"Perfect" responds Stacey

The next Thursday Bar night at Jacomelli's proves to be an eye opener ... Gez arrives and is greeted by Janet on the door ...

"It was a fabulous night, last Saturday" advises Janet (Smiling)

"Yes, I loved every minute of it" replies Jenny (a green eyed brunette)

"Are you up for another, honey?" asks Jackie
"Well OK, I'm up for it, if you are" replies Gez (Laughing)

"I thoroughly enjoyed myself on Saturday too" explains Gez
Various members come forward to talk to Gez about the party at the Green ...
"Hi, I'm Geof ... I really enjoyed your party" advises Geof (Shakes hands)
"OH, thanks, Geof"
replies Gez
"I was wondering"
asks Geof
"Yes?" replies Gez
"If you'd be interested in an old Tandy 60s double turntable,and a single speaker ... we used to use it for the scouts ... you can have the lot for £15" advises Geof
"Geof, that's fabulous ... I'll take it" replies Gez (Laughing) Both shake hands!
"OK, you'll have to collect it from my flat in Baildon" advises Geof
"No problem, we'll arrange it between us"

replies Gez

Gez additionally buys another speaker, microphone and tape deck from Tandy. Gez has a mate give the unit the once over.

The deck with it's primitive electrics are OK, and it does the job …

Gez arranges another party on 14th April … The Mad Hatter's Party. This time with another member, Terry, and again at the Green Community Centre.

We charged more for a buffet, and it became another SOLD OUT event, but there were problems …

"Where's Terry tonight?" asks Gez

(Looking anxious)

"No where to be seen" replies Danny

"I've made a big mistake tonight, Danny" advises Gez

"Not only has Terry not shown, but we've only 70 members here and we booked the buffet for 100" explains Gez (Looks concerned)

"But I still have to pay for

100" advises Gez

Terry eventually turned up

at 11pm!

"Thanks for getting here"

advises Gez

"Sorry, I was otherwise detained" adds Terry

"I bet you were … what was she called?" asks Gez

The next Bar night in Leeds proved to be rather interesting ... Gez is greeted by Janet on arrival ...
"Thank you for another enjoyable evening, Gez" advises Janet (Smiling)
"Sorry, I couldn't make it ... did everything go well?" asks Janet
"Well, Janet ... I made two mistakes" replies Gez
"Why, what happened?" asks Janet
"Firstly, Terry was no where to be seen, and secondly the buffet catered for a hundred but we only had seventy members attend" explains Gez
"Never again ... I was out of pocket" advises Gez

"Events will go on, but there will be no more buffets or joint parties ... I'll do them on my own" replies Gez
"I think your right, Terry is really quite unreliable" replies Janet (Looks concerned)

"His days are numbered ... we've had lots of complaints about him" explains Janet
"I've been thinking of doing something on a grand scale" advises Gez (Smiling)
"Really, what have you got in mind, Gez" asks Janet (Smiling)
"Something for the ITV Telethon 90" explains Gez

"What if we do a discoathon at the Green Community Centre on Bank Holiday Monday, 28th

May?" adds Gez (Smiling)
"We could sell tickets in advance for £1 each, making all proceeds to Telethon" explains Gez (Smiling)
"How does it sound, Janet?"
asks Gez
"Wonderful … can it be
done?" replies Janet

"Sure, if we pull this off then who knows what's next" enthuses Gez

Danny and Dave now enter the Bar area at Jacomelli's in Leeds ...

"Danny ... are you up for the Telethon?" asks Gez

"Count me in, Gez" replies Danny (Laughing)

"Me, too" replies Dave (Laughing)

"Perfect ... I can't do it all on my own" advises Gez (Laughing)

"Everyone in Mirage can help too" explains Gez

"OK ... I'm in contact with Yorkshire Television ... we'll see if we can get a celebrity, to join us on the day" advises Gez (Looks excited)

"It really sounds fabulous" replies Janet

Gez returns home and decides to contact Yorkshire Television next day ... Gez makes a telephone call ...

"My name is Gez. I'm putting on an event with lots of others over the Bank Holiday weekend" advises Gez

"How can we help you?" asks a female TV Executive

"I was wondering, do you have anyone we could have as a celebrity guest?" asks Gez

"As a matter of fact we do ... we can let you have Tony Star" explains the Executive

"Who?" replies Gez (Puzzled)

"He's a local Tom Cruise lookalike"

advises the Executive

"Perfect … we'll take him" answers Gez (Excited)

Telethon Day arrives and it couldn't have been more perfect … luckily it was a hot sunny day … just right for everything we had planned …

DJ Dave gets the show on the road and makes announcements over the loud speaker system to passers by and the public in Horsforth …

"OK, we now have local dancers to entertain us … if you look across the way" adds Dave

It's a young troupe of dancers … they begin to perform to the Irish music provided by Dave.

"Who's that dressed in drag?" asks Dave (Laughing)

"No idea, mate" replies Danny (Laughing)

"Oh, it's Jason" advises Gez (Laughing)

"Well, he looks good as a woman" laughs Dave

"Oh, he's collecting money for Telethon" explains Gez (Laughing)

Danny is dressed as a character from a film …

"Wow, Danny … look at you" laughs Gez

"Oh, I'm the Incredible Hulk" advises Danny (Laughing)

"It must have taken you hours to get ready" adds Gez (Laughing)

"How did you do it?" asks Dave (Laughing)
"Oh, it's all green fluid for baking … I'll have to have several baths to wash it off" explains Danny (All Laughing)
"You look so macho" advises Sarah (Big Smile)

"Hey, she's showing her knickers" advises DJ Dave to the crowds (Laughing)

"Who is?" asks Sarah (Looks stunned)
"Oh, it's only Jason … giving us all a flash" laughs Gez

"Any road it's all being done in the name of a good cause" advises Gez

"Your a true sport, Danny" adds Gez (Laughing)
"Dave, what do you think of Danny" asks Gez
"A right plonker" replies Dave (All Laughing)

We had a schedule of events from 10am to Midnight … We had arranged to meet Tony Star at Leeds City Station … At the entrance to the station next to the Queens Hotel …
A smart young man in sun glasses walks towards us …
"Wow Yorkshire TV were right you do look like Tom Cruise" advises Gez (Smiling)
"Hi, I'm Tony" greets lookalike Tom (All shaking hands)
'I'm Gez … this is Danny" advises Gez (Smiling)

Gez is dressed in the official Telethon 90 sweatshirt … Danny, is of course, the Hulk …

Everyone at Leeds City Station was staring at Tony. He really did look like Tom Cruise ...
"You look exactly like who you say you are" advises Tony (Laughing)
"The spitting image" replies Gez (Laughing)
"I can stay with you till say 8pm, then I'll have to catch my train home" advises Tony (Smiling)
"OK, Tony, that's fine ... we'll pay for your train fare" explains Gez

We had a series of Events at the Green, with Tony as ambassador. It was an on the day collection by means of buckets from passing cars, the public, and going round the pubs in Horsforth to raise money for Telethon ... we raised £703!!!
We had a large Bank presentation cheque made out to Yorkshire Television Telethon 90.
We all made the journey by car to Yorkshire Television studios on Kirkstall Road ...
We presented our cheque to several members of the Emmerdale cast. A TV producer guided us throughout the proceedings ...
"Follow the Yellow Brick Road" advises the TV producer

"Tall gentlemen at the back, please" explains another producer

Tony Star was given pride of place, at the front of our photo shoot.
It was a fabulous day. Tony left to catch his train home. Everyone else at Mirage decided to opt for our special evening of dance and music at the Green.

After such a big occasion … Gez decides to take a break from Mirage for several weeks.
Gez then decides to go back to Tapas …

A new door man is in place to meet and greet all members …

"Hi, I'm Gerry … how are you?" asks a voice
Gerry is tall and slim, has grey hair, works for the Inland Revenue in Leeds …
"Hi, I'm Gez … glad to meet you" (Smiling)
Gez enters Tapas Bar area …

"Hey, look what the cat's dragged in" advises Mike (Laughing)

"Where have you been?" asks Ernest (Looks concerned)
"Oh, doing this and that, you know" replies Gez (Smiling)

"Your old girlfriend, Jane … has got herself engaged" advises Ernest (Laughing)

"Oh … she was never my girlfriend, Ernest … we were just good friends" replies Gez (Smiling)
"Friends with benefits?" asks
Mike (Laughing)
"Yea, something like that"
replies Gez (Laughing)
Gerry, the doorman walks over to the bar …

"So, Gerry … have you got your eye on anyone here?" asks Mike (Smiling)
"Oh … you see Pam … the blonde?"

replies Gerry (Smiling)
"Oh, yea … I see" advises Mike (Looks across the room)
"Lucky you" adds Ernest (Laughing)
"Oh, no … we're just good friends, mate … she's seeing someone else" explains Gerry (Smiling)
"What, and not you … she doesn't know what she's missing" adds Mike (Laughing)
Gerry goes back to the door area to greet incoming members …
"He still carries a torch for her" explains Mike
"So, Gezza what the heck have you been up to?" asks Mike (Laughing)

"I don't suppose you would believe me if I told you I was a trappist monk?" replies Gez (Smiling)
"Too right" adds Mike (Laughing)

"What's on this weekend?" asks Gez (Smiling)

"Oh, a Back to School Party in Pudsey … do you want to go?" asks Mike

"Oh, yea, I'm up for it, Mike" advises Gez (Laughing)
"What about you Ernest?" asks Gez (Laughing)

"Ernest's going as one of the teachers" explains Mike (Laughing)

"And what are we going as?" asks Gez (Laughing)
"Naughty school boys, of course" replies Mike (Laughing)

"We'll soon knock those girls into shape"
quips Mike (Laughing)
"Bet they missed me?" asks Gez (Smiling)
"Oh, there's more for you to go at now, lad" advises Ernest (Laughing)
Saturday arrives, Mike, Gez and Ernest arrive at the Back to School party … Mike turns up as himself …

"Hi, Mike … I see you've dressed for the occasion … what have you come as?" asks Gez (Smiling)
"Oh, me, naturally … they will have to take me as I am" replies Mike (Laughing)
"Oh, wow … look over there" adds Mike (Pointing)
"There's lots of tiny skirts, stockings and suspenders, all over the place" explains Mike (Laughing)
"Come on Gezza … it's time to introduce ourselves" adds Mike (Laughing)

Gez and Mike begin to mingle …

"Hi, we're Mike and Gez … we're the meet and greeters at Tapas" advises Mike

"Well, hello to you both" greets a voice (Sexy)
"I'm Tara … and that's Simone" replies
the voice (Big Smile)
"We like your outfits, love" advises
Mike (Smiling)
"We thought you might" replies Simone (Smiling)

"We put a lot of thought into it … the shorter the better" explains Tara (Smiling)

"Well, you do have legs that go right up to your bum, love" quips Mike (Laughing)
"Come on, Tara … you've pulled" laughs Mike

"Looks like you have too, Simone" replies Gez (Laughing)

Ernest enters the party …

"Do you come here often, love?" asks
Mike (Laughing)

"Only if your here" replies Tara (Big Smile)
"What a stunner" advises Ernest (Laughing)
"What you think of mine?" asks Gez (Laughing)
"Two stunners" beams Ernest
"There's plenty for you, pal" quips Mike (Laughing)
The party goes into dancing mode … and the DJ is playing lots of old stuff to get everyone on the dance floor …
"Oh, I love this" advises Simone (Smiling)
"Yea, it's a good one" replies Gez (Laughing)
The dance floor is perched above a downstairs bar … Suddenly, Mike notices something …
Two men begin to climb up to the balcony …

"Hey, what are you blokes doing … climbing up here?" shouts Mike (Looks concerned)

Both men don't reply …
"Oh, I get it … they can see right up your skirts" advises Mike (Smiling)
"Well, the skirts are short" adds Ernest (Laughing)
"Sorry, it had to be done … I couldn't take it much longer" advises a bloke in the bar
"Well, at least they have got great taste" adds Mike (Laughing)

"I take it, your both wearing knickers?"
asks Mike

"What a thing to ask" replies Tara (Smiling)

"Otherwise we'd have to take down your particulars" quips Mike (Laughing)

"That's knickers to you, love" explains Ernest (Laughing)
"Your so naughty" replies Simone (Smiling)

"Naughty by name … and naughty by nature" advises Mike (Laughing)

"That's us" adds Gez (Laughing)
"And you two are supposed to be the meet and greeters at Tapas?" asks Tara (Laughing)
"We sure are, love" replies Mike (Laughing)

"I bet your both glad you met us, aren't you?" adds Gez (Laughing)
"Tara and Simone, stay by us … we'll look after your assets" quips Mike (Laughing)
"You did say assets?" asks Tara (Smiling)

"Your both smooth talkers" replies Simone (Smiling)

"Are you both brothers?" asks Tara (Smiling)
"Only partners in crime" adds Mike (Laughing)
"Are you the cops?" asks Simone (Smiling)
"No … are you the fuzz?" replies Mike (All Laughing)

IF MUSIC BE THE FOOD OF LOVE

It's almost Halloween ... Tuesday Bar night at Tapas, Lower Briggate, Leeds ... Gez and Mike are in conversation in the Bar area ...
"I see another party is on the cards, this weekend, Mike" advises Gez (Smiling)
"What is it?" asks Mike (Laughing)
"A Halloween party in Huddersfield ... fancy going?" asks Gez (Points to Events Board near Bar)

"Aye lad, count me in ... I could do with a good fright" replies Mike (Laughing)

"Oh, very funny" quips Gez (Smiling)
"Are you going to dress up for it?"
asks Gez (Laughing)
"Don't I always" replies Mike (Laughing)
"No, that's just it ... you don't" advises Gez (Smiling)
"There you go then" adds Mike (Laughing)
Ernest enters Tapas and wanders over to Mike and Gez ...

"Ernest will do us proud though ... won't you?" asks Mike (Smiling)

"I'll dress up if you will" advises Ernest

(Laughing)
"OK, mate do it" replies Gez
"And I'll do it too" explains Gez (Laughing)
"That's settled, then" replies Mike (Laughing)
The weekend of the Halloween party
in Huddersfield arrives … Mike and Gez
arrive together …
"What have you come as?" asks Mike (Laughing)

"Oh, Count Rockula, Phantom of the Rock Opera, rising again on Halloween" advises Gez (Laughing)
"You look a sight" laughs Mike
"Well, you should've stopped in your grave"
adds Mike (Laughing)
"Infamy … infamy" shouts Gez (Laughing)
"Ah, the old Kenneth Williams, line" replies Mike
(Laughing)

"Yea, that's just it … in for me … they've all got it
in for me" shouts Gez (Laughing)
"Well, you asked for it" adds Gez

"Very funny, Gezza" replies Mike (Both Laughing)

"I see you've come as your usual self" adds Gez
(Smiling)

Mike is dressed in a white shirt complete
with black trousers …

"See, I told you, this is my party gear"
laughs Mike
"I don't do fancy dress, mate" replies Mike
(Laughing)

A rather classy lady walks over to

talk to Mike and Gez ...

"Hi, I'm Pam ... I love your outfit"
advises Pam (Big Smile)

"Your outfit's not bad either, love"
quips Gez (Smiling)
Pam is a tall leggy blonde, has green eyes and a full on figure ...
"See, what fancy dress can do for you, Mike?" adds Gez (Laughing)
"Well, your doing nothing for me ... that's it" replies Mike (Laughing)
Suddenly in pops the scourge of
Zodiac ... Rick ...
"Hey, it looks like Rick has just arrived" advises Gez
"Oh, no he hasn't has he?" asks
Mike (Looks serious)
"No ... we were just pulling your leg"
quips Gez (Laughing)
Mike looks relieved ...
Suddenly the host of the party wanders over to meet Mike and Gez ...
"Hi ... I'm James ... welcome to our party"
greets the voice
"I'm Mike and that's Gezza ... we're both from Leeds"
quips Mike (Laughing)
James has gone to great lengths with his costume for Halloween ...
"Oh, James ... your outfit's incredible"
advises Gez (Laughing)

James is dressed in bandages from head to foot and covered in fake blood …

"Hey, does your Mummy know?" quips Mike (Laughing)

"Oh, very witty" replies James (Laughing)

"I'm thinking of having a party in the New Year" advises Gez (Smiling)

"So look out for it" explains Gez

"Oh, we will, mate … we like a boogie or two" advises James (Laughing)

"Any way I have to go now … and get into the spirit of things" quips James

"Oh, very funny" replies Mike (Laughing)

Suddenly two other voices greet

Mike and Gez …

"Hi … we're Linda and Natalie"

says a voice

Linda is a slim brunette, has a beaming smile and very curvy … Natalie is in her thirties, has short brown hair, green eyes and quite attractive …

"Hi, we're Mike and Gez from Leeds"

quips Mike (Smiling)

"We like your outfit's, love" explains

Mike (Laughing)

Both girls are dressed as witches in

very short skirts …

"Thanks, Mike" replies Linda (Smiling)

"What about you, honey?" asks Natalie (Big Smile)

"Has the witches cat got your tongue, love?"

explains Natalie (Laughing)

"Oh, I'm spell bound, love" quips Gez (Laughing)
Natalie is a picture in her mini, make up
and Halloween outfit …
"Do you like my outfit, Gez?" asks Natalie
(Big Smile)
"Absolutely … it's the tops honey" replies
Gez (Laughing)
"Well, if you play your cards right, tonight" adds Natalie
"Will you be my dolly dealer?"
asks Gez (Laughing)
"Naturally"explains Natalie
(Laughing)
Suddenly the music changes from Halloween
tunes to a 60s mix …
"Hey, this isn't Halloween, it's a 60s song"
advises Mike
"Yea, but it's very apt, Mike" replies Gez (Laughing)

At the next Bar Night at Tapas, Mike and Gez are the talk of the night …

"You do know they are all talking about us, don't you Mike?" asks Gez (Looks concerned)

"Oh, let them" quips Mike (Laughing)
"We're only human" adds Mike (Laughing)

"I say we're only human" shouts Mike (Very Loudly)

Ernest enters Tapas and moves over to Mike and Gez in the bar area …

"Good on you both" quips Ernest (Laughing)

"And, where were you Ernest, on Saturday?" asks Mike (Smiling)

"Oh, I was there … but I spent most of the night in the kitchen with a blonde" explains Ernest (Laughing)
"Yea … that figures" adds Mike (Laughing)

Mike, Gez and Ernest check out the Events board next to the bar …

"What's up next?" asks Gez
"Oh, a Doctor's and Nurses Party in Leeds" advises Mike (Smiling)
"We're all going to that on Saturday" advises Mike
"Sure thing, Mike" replies Gez (Laughing)

"It's practically on your own turf, Mike" replies Ernest (Laughing)

"Yea, Ernest … not far to go" quips Mike (Smiling)
Gez advises Mike that he has several white Doctor's type coats in his possession …
"I'll bring you a white coat, just like a Doctor's, Mike" advises Gez (Smiling)
"Will it fit me, Gezza?" asks Mike (Smiling)
"Hopefully" replies Gez (Laughing)

Saturday arrives, Mike and Gez meet and arrive at the venue … there are already quite a few sights to be seen …
Gez hands Mike a white Doctor
type of coat …

"Does it fit, Mike" asks Gez
Mike dons the white coat …

"Perfect fit, mate" replies Mike (Laughing)

"Thought it would … it's a very large one" explains Gez (Laughing)

"Cheeky" adds Mike (Laughing)
"I'm Doctor Get them off, tonight,
Mike" laughs Gez
"Do you get it, Mike?" asks Gez (Laughing)
"We'll all get it tonight, mate, if you know what I mean" replies Mike (Laughing)
"There are lots of nurses scantily dressed here, tonight" explains Gez (Smiling)
"Yea, we're both in our element" replies Mike (Laughing)
"Remember the Zodiac code?"
advises Gez (Smiling)
"Is there a Doctor in the house"
quips Mike (Laughing)
Mike motions to Gez …

"I think that brassy blonde woman in the Barbara Windsor outfit is wanting some attention" advises Mike (Laughing)
"I think I'll leave that one to you, Mike" replies Gez (Laughing)
"It's virtually being offered, on a plate" quips Mike (Laughing)
"Where's Ernest?" asks Gez (Smiling)
A woman called Patsy now enters the scene …

"Hey, she's just grabbed my back side … and more than once" advises Gez (Laughing)
"Who?" asks Mike (Looks stunned)

"Patsy has just grabbed my bottom" replies Gez (Laughing)

"Well what are you complaining about, enjoy it while you can" advises Ernest (Laughing)

"Well, go and grab hers" advises Mike (Laughing)
"Then, she'll know your interested" laughs Mike
Some of the girls, at the party, didn't like Patsy and they took delight in advising Gez that she was up for anything …
A young woman, with wavy brunette hair takes Gez by the hand …
"Gez, a word in your ear, love" advises Kate (Big Smile)
"Take care, she's the club bike" explains Kate

"Oh, I get it … I'd rather be with you, Kate" replies Gez (Smiling)

"Oh, thanks love … come and dance" advises Kate (Big Smile)

"Besides you've got lovely legs" adds Gez (Laughing)
"Thanks, love" replies Kate (Big Smile)

Meanwhile, back at Mirage … all the talk is of the Christmas disco at Jacomelli's …

Early Thursday evening, Gez meets Danny in the Bar area …

"Hi Danny … how are you, mate?" asks Gez

"Great, just great" replies Danny (Smiling)

"Are you going to the Christmas disco at the Green this weekend?" asks Danny

"Oh, yes I am … what about you?" replies Gez

"Just got my ticket … they are selling like hot cakes, tonight" laughs Danny

"Is Dave providing the music?" asks Gez

"Oh, yea, Dave will be doing the honours ... and well, we'll be free to mingle" explains Danny (Laughing)
"Mingle and jingle" replies Gez (Laughing)

The night of the Christmas disco arrives ... everyone is dressed up to the nines at the Green Community Centre in Horsforth ...
Danny and Gez join DJ Dave in the main room ...
"We're all like family here" advises Dave
"Oh, yea, everyone's bonding together" laughs Danny
Dave starts to play Hot Stuff by Donna Summer ...
"Hi, I'm Cathy" says a voice

Cathy is a slim, dark haired woman, and has bewitching eyes ...

"Hi, I'm Gez" replies Gez (Smiling)
"Oh, I know who you are ... and your going to dance with me, aren't you?" asks Cathy (Big Smile)
"OK, Cathy, lets get on the dance floor" replies Gez (Laughing)

Now, Cathy was a slim attractive brunette, and another Cockney, but she had a chequered past ... Another member called Peter had been taking her out and he was still besotted by her ... they were once an item!

Peter is tall, has dark hair and obviously has something for Cathy ...
"Oh, don't worry about him" advises Cathy
"I'm no one's property" explains Cathy (Smiling)

Still Gez feels uncomfortable, as Peter is also a friend ...

"Let's have another glass of wine" asks Cathy
"Well, it is almost Christmas" advises Gez (Smiling)
Cathy asks to go back on the dance floor ...

"Danny, it's your turn ... he'll join you OK?" advises Gez (Laughing)

"OK" replies Danny (Smiling)
Cathy goes on to the dance floor with Danny ...

"Go on Danny, do your stuff" advises Gez (Laughing)

After a few dances, Danny retreats from the dance floor ...

"She's got form, Danny" advises Gez
"Form?" replies Danny (Looks puzzled)

"Oh, she used to go out with Peter" explains Danny (Laughing)

"Yea, and he's here tonight ... he gives me the creeps" explains Gez (Smiling)

"Just avoid him ... Pete's OK, I think he's smitten with Cathy" advises Danny

"Your not wrong there, Danny" laughs Gez
"I'm planning more Events next year" advises Gez

"Can you help me in future, Danny?" explains Gez
"Yea, I'd love to" quips Danny (Laughing)
"I'll be doing more here and at Zodiac" advises Gez (Laughing)
"But I'm not a member there" replies Danny
"I think you will be, when you see what talent's available" laughs Gez
"You'll be like a kid in a sweet shop" explains Gez (Both Laughing)
"You will really be spoilt for choice" adds Gez (Laughing)
"OK, count me in, I'll join" advises Danny (Laughing)

It's the end of the Christmas disco, and everyone begins to leave the Green Community Centre … Danny and Gez suddenly look out of the upstairs window … "See what I see?" asks Danny
Gez looks out of the window …

"Oh, yea … I'm so glad I decided not to do anything" replies Gez

It was only Peter trailing behind Cathy, like some love sick teenager!

"Well, it takes all types, I guess" laughs Gez
"There's a Hair of the Dog party in Lawnswood on Boxing day … do you fancy going, Gezza?" asks Danny (Smiling)
"Yea, OK … I'll be there" replies Gez (Smiling)

"Are you doing anything for New Year's Eve?" asks Danny

"Well, there's a Zodiac party in Wakefield" replies Gez

"Do you want to come, Danny?" asks Gez
"Will it be OK?" asks Danny

"I'll get a couple of tickets, you can try it out" advises Gez (Laughing)

"OK, I don't mind if I do, pal" replies Danny (Laughing)
"Is it a Fancy dress do?" asks Danny

"Yea, it's a Cowboy's and Indian's party" explains Gez

"Sounds good to me, lets go for it, partner" quips Danny (Laughing)

"Oh, very funny, Daniel" laughs Gez
It's now New Year's Eve and Gez and Danny arrive at the party venue, dressed for the occasion …
"Hey, I like your gear, Danny" laughs Gez

Danny is decked out in a cowboy hat and waist coat with typical shirt and neck scarf, he has a double gun belt, and wearing a tin star …
"You'll be the sheriff, then?"
asks Gez (Laughing)
Gez is also decked out in very
similar gear … "Hey, just look at
you, Danny" adds Gez
"You, look good too, mate"

laughs Danny
"We'll ring all their bells
tonight" adds Gez
The music starts up and several ladies are now on the dance floor …

Gez and Danny notice two young ladies and decide to move in for a dance … "Can we join you?" asks Danny (Smiling)
"Hi, we're Danny and Gez"
explains Danny
"Oh, Terri and Sally" replies
Terri (Big Smile)
Both are good lookers, and quite attractive …

"We're here to round up all the fillies" explains Danny (Laughing)

"That's us … we'll be your fillies" replies Sally (Smiling)
"You two can ring our bells anytime"
adds Terri (Big Smile)
"Sweet talking girl" laughs Danny
"Do you want to climb on my horse?"
asks Danny (Laughing)
"Wow … your a bit forward, aren't you?" replies Terri (Laughing)
"Yea, I'm always going forwards … not backwards" quips Danny
"Pardon?" asks Sally (Looks stunned)
"Oh, he's had two many sarsaparilla's" explains Gez (Smiling)
"Get off your horse and drink your

milk" adds Gez (Laughing)
"OK, partner" replies Danny (Laughing)
"Are you fillies up for a drink?" asks
Gez (Smiling)
"Take us by the hand, and lead us
there" replies Terri (Smiling)
"We've got two ravers tonight"
laughs Danny
"Oh yea … and both have got legs up to
their …" quips Danny
"Danny are you OK, mate?" asks Gez
(Looks concerned)
"I think I've had one over the eight" explains Danny
"Well, you do look a bit green" replies Gez

"Hey, your not turning into the green eyed monster are you?" laughs Gez

It's almost Midnight, everyone takes to the dance floor …
"Your wish is my command" quips Danny

"Danny, your sozzled" replies Gez
(Looks really concerned)

"Who's birthday is it?" asks Danny
"Danny, it's New Year's Eve" advises Gez

"Hey, don't go all funny on me now" adds Gez

"Here's Terri and Sally … remember them?" asks Gez (Still concerned)

"Right … let the countdown begin" shouts someone
"Five … four … three … two … one"

adds Gez (Smiling) "Happy New Year"
shout everyone
Lots of kissing and hugging takes place …
and that's just Danny!
"Well, were into 1991 now, Dan" advises
Gez (Laughing)
Both shake hands …

"Yea, I wonder what all this year will bring?" asks Danny

"One things for sure … if we both play our cards right" adds Gez

"Oh, yea … we've pulled here" explains
Gez
"Are you glad you came, Danny?"
asks Gez (Laughing)
"I sure am, partner" replies Danny
(All Laughing)

CLOSE ENCOUNTERS OF … THE FEMALE KIND!

Gez is in conversation with Mike and Ernest in the Bar area of Tapas …

"I recently had my palm read" advises Gez
"Did they ask you to cross their palms with silver?" laughs Mike

"Well, yea, as a matter of fact she did, I had to pay for the reading, if that's what you mean" replies Gez (Laughing)

"There's one born, every minute" quips Ernest (Laughing)

"Come on, Gezza … what advice did she give you?" asks Mike (Smiling)

"She told me, I had a lot of admirers" replies Gez
"Well, I could have told you that, for nothing" adds Ernest (Laughing)
"What did you say?" asks Mike (Looks interested)
"I told her, I was lost for words" explains Gez

"She then said it was true … that good fortune was going to smile on me" adds Gez
"And that I was a magnet for all females" laughs Gez

"See, we told you that, yonks ago"
adds Mike (Laughing)
"Where did you get all this information?" asks Ernest (Looks puzzled)
"From a gypsy in Blackpool" quips Gez (Smiling)
"I suppose it was Gypsy Rosa Lee?"
asks Mike (Laughing)
"Well, yes, as a matter of fact, it was"
replies Gez
"Perhaps she may be right, Gezza"
laughs Mike
"Let's hope so" laughs Ernest

"So what's happening, Gezza?" asks Mike

"I've arranged, my first Zodiac event" advises Gez (Smiling)
"Good on you, Gezza" replies Mike (Looks excited)
"Your a dark horse, where and when?" asks Mike (Looks intrigued)

"Oh, it's on Saturday 31st of March, at a private function room at CJ's Bar in Heckmondwike" replies Gez (Smiling)
"Have you told, David?" asks Mike (Looks puzzled)

"Oh, yea … he's going to put it in the bulletin" explains Gez (Smiling)

"I'm just doing the advertising … it'll be on the board soon" advises Gez (Looks pleased)

"What's it going to be?" asks Mike (Looks intrigued)

"Oh, I've called it … A Celebration Disco … and I'll do it in two sets" explains Gez (Smiling)
"First set will be rock and roll, and the second set will be more up to date stuff" advises Gez
"I've also booked, my mate, Harry … he'll be performing various electronic guitar hits live on stage" adds Gez (Smiling)
"My, you have been busy" quips
Ernest (Laughing)
"Wow, it sounds fabulous, Gezza"
advises Mike (Looks excited)
"Just what we need in Leeds … you'll do us proud if you can pull it off" explains Mike (Smiling)
"That sounds great, lad" advises Ernest (Smiling)

"Oh, thanks, Ernest … I never do the easy option" replies Gez (Smiling)

"Will it work?" asks Mike (Looks concerned)
"Yes, of course it will, Mike … now all of you can help me, OK?" asks Gez
"Yes, count us both in" replies Mike
Suddenly, more new members arrive at Tapas …

"Go on, Gezza … these two look to be right up your street" advises Mike (Smiling)
"OK, Mike … I'll see to them" replies Gez (Smiling)

Gez meanders over to the two young ladies …

"Hi, I'm Gez … I'm a meeter and greet with Mike" advises Mike

"That's Mike over there" explains Gez (Pointing)

"Hello, girls" adds Mike (Smiling)

"Hi, I'm Carla … this is Sally … we're both nurses at Leeds General Infirmary" explains Carla (Big Smile)
"And stunners too" quips Gez (Smiling)

"Why, thank you, kind Sir" replies Sally (Big Smile)

Carla is five foot seven, has long brown hair, and very attractive. Sally is five foot six, has blonde curly hair … both are single and in their early thirties …
"You have beautiful blue eyes, Sally" adds Gez (Big Smile)

"Oh, thanks … one of my outstanding features" replies Sally (Smiling)

"What about me?" asks Carla
"Oh, your very attractive, too" explains Gez

"Well, I can think of two others" advises Mike (Laughing)

"Cheeky" replies Carla
"Oh, I'm helping Mike … we're the resident welcomers at Tapas" advises Gez
"OK, have a look at our Events board, near the bar … see what's on … we'll have a dance later" explains Gez (Smiling)
"Oh, we'll be back for that, love" adds Carla (Big Smile)
"I bet you will" adds Ernest (Laughing)
"You see, you've got them eating out of your hands already" advises Ernest (Laughing)
"Yes, but I've only just met them" replies Gez

(Smiling)
"Steady on ... he's just winding you up" advises Mike (Laughing)

Gez and Mike continue to meet and greet new members to Tapas ... Carla comes over to Gez, who is now close to the bar, with Mike and Ernest ...

"There's a Space Age party in Pudsey on Saturday" advises Carla (Beaming)

"Fancy going?" asks Carla (Smiling)

"Well be there, love" replies Mike (Laughing)

"Oh, well I'm definitely going then" adds Carla (Big Smile)

The DJ changes the music to disco ...

"Well, girls are we on the dance floor or what?" asks Gez (Smiling)

"What?" asks Sally (Smiles)
"Lead on" replies Carla (Smiling)

Carla does some sort of funny turn around routine as a wake up call to see if Gez is interested ...
"That was kind of cute, Carla" advises Gez (Smiling)

"Just to see if you are interested?" replies Carla (Big Smile)

"Yes, of course I am" explains Gez (Laughing)
"Hey, are you girls coming to my party?" asks Gez (Looks pleased)
"When is it?" asks Sally

"Saturday week on the 31st of March" explains Gez

"Are you both free?" asks Gez
(Smiles)
"Yea, we're not on duty then"
advises Carla (Beaming)
"Perfect" adds Gez (Looks happy)
"What kind of party is it, Gez?" asks Sally (Smiling)

"Oh, it's my first one for Zodiac … it's called A Celebration Disco" explains Gez

"First half rock and roll, second half more up to date stuff" advises Gez (Smiling)
"Well, are you coming?" asks Gez

"Quite the entertainer, aren't you, love"
advises Carla (Big smile)

"Well, have you both got tickets?" asks Gez
"No, but when we do … you can punch our tickets" replies Sally (Big Smile)
"What a thing to say … and I've only just met you" adds Gez (Looks stunned)
"Well, wait until you really get to know us" laughs Sally

Gez remembers the old Roger Moore charm, and it worked to a tee! Saturday evening … the night of the Space Age party …
Carla and Sally are already there …

Gez arrives at the event and is greeted by Carla …

"You look good tonight, Carla, in your nice but short outfit" quips Gez

"I thought you'd like it, love" replies Carla

(Smiling)
"Are you always this flirty?" asks Gez (Smiling)
"Only with you, love" replies Carla (Big Smile)
Rick, as in prick, arrives ... Carla seems to be taken in by his style! She really didn't have great taste ... off putting or what?
Ernest arrives on the scene and notes that Rick is chatting up Carla ...
"I see prick's arrived" laughs Ernest
"Yea, and he's got a one way ticket out of here" adds Gez (Laughing)
"Luckily, Mike isn't here tonight, Ernest" adds Gez
Meanwhile, at the next bar night in Tapas, Mike is being brought up to speed by Ernest and Gez with regards the party ...
"How did it go on, Saturday?" asks Mike
"Oh, fine ... but" replies Gez
"But what?" asks Mike
"Oh our old mate, prick ... I mean Rick turned up" advises Gez
"What happened?" asks Mike
"Oh, Carla, the new brunette seemed to be taken in by him" advises Gez (Looks puzzled)
"Just a flash in the pan ... look she's here tonight" adds Mike (Pointing)
"Yea, she'll be after your body again"

advises Ernest (Laughing)
"Oh, thanks, Ernest" replies Gez (Laughing)
Tapas starts to fill up with old and new members. Someone comes over to Gez asking for tickets …
"Can we have tickets for your do?" asks a voice

"Oh, sorry … it was sold out 3 weeks ago … and we can't take any more due to the venues restrictions" advises Gez
"We've about 200 coming … but I will be putting on a follow up later in the year" explains Gez
"I'm so sorry, but it's all down to numbers and regulations" advises Gez
Gez turns to Mike …
"Boy, I could have sold tickets three times over" advises Gez (Smiling)
"Your putting us the entertainment map" quips Mike (Laughing)
"There's a lot more to come … this is just the beginning" replies Gez
"See what you've done" advises Ernest
"What I've done?" asks Gez (Looks concerned)

"Well, what Ernest means, is that everything is in overdrive now" adds Mike (Laughing)
"Long may it continue … I'm so glad for you, Gezza" laughs Mike

"Yea … see what's happened to you since joining Zodiac" adds Ernest

"Your cemented in Zodiac history, already"

explains Mike (Laughing)
"Well, what an honour" replies Gez (Smiling)

Saturday of the Celebration Disco arrives … it's the beginning of everything! Gez arrives early and sets up the twin decks and speaker system. A new tape deck and microphone is also added to the show …
Lots of members are now congregating in the upstairs private suite at CJ's Bar …

It's just after 8.30pm … Gez dims the lights …

"Hi, Welcome to CJ's and to our Celebration Disco" advises Gez

Lots of applause from Zodiac members …
"We'll have the first set of rock and roll followed by the second set of more up to date stuff, finally we'll end with a love songs compilation" advises Gez (Smiling)
"Are you all ready to move it?"
asks Gez (Laughing)
The rock n rollers are in their element …
Ernest arrives on the scene …

"Now where are all the girls … let me get at them" laughs Ernest

Mike joins Gez at the Disco console …
"We'll have to keep an eye on him tonight, Gezza" advises Mike
Lots of rock and roll songs are played …
Half an hour into the evening … Gez makes an

announcement …

"OK, it's time for our Live set with Harry playing instrumentals" explains Gez (Smiling)

Harry starts to a round of applause … but it's not long before gremlins infiltrate his sound and equipment …
"Sorry, mate I'll have to do
it again" advises Harry (Looks
embarrassed)
"OK, we'll start it again" replies
Gez
Gez leans over to Harry …
"Just mime to it … they'll never know the difference … I'll put a record on … go when I tell you OK?" asks Gez
"OK, I'll do it" replies Harry (Smiles)

Gez plays several guitar instrumentals … Harry mimes to them … it all goes down well with the Zodiac members …
Ernest comes over to Mike and
Gez for a chat …
"Look at all the pussy in here
tonight" advises Ernest
"We're talking pussy" adds Ernest
(Laughing)
"I can't see any cats"
laughs Gez
"Oh, very funny"
laughs Ernest
Suddenly, Carla and Sally start to dance in

front of the disco console …
"Are you going to dance with me?" asks Carla (Big Smile)
"OK, Carla, yes let's go for it" adds Gez (Smiling)
"We're both up for it, love" advises Sally (Smiling)
"Do you want any help?" asks Danny
"Yea, can you mind the shop for me, Danny?" asks Gez (Laughing)
"It would be an honour, mate" laughs Danny

Ernest is now talking to Mike …
"He's a lucky man, Mike" advises Ernest

"He sure is Ernest, have you got your eye on anyone" asks Mike

"Oh, there's that blonde over there" replies Ernest

"Oh, she's mine" explains Mike (Laughing)

"Well, she doesn't know it yet … but she will do soon" advises Mike (Smiling)

Gez plays more upbeat pop music with a mix from the 70s and 80s …

"This one's especially for Ernest" announces Gez (All Laughing)
"Groovy baby" replies Ernest (Laughing)

"Just look at him … he looks a proper nana" advises Mike (All Laughing)

Ernest blows them all away with his one man show …

Next up, it's the love songs section …

Carla comes over to Gez and makes her presence known …

"It's time for a smooch, love" advises Carla (Winking)

"What about me?" asks Sally
"Oh, I'll dance with you, love" replies Danny (Smiling)

After a few smoochy dances with Carla, it's back to business for Gez and the end of the night …
Gez stops the music to make a few announcements …

"I just want to thank a few people tonight … Mike, for his belief and encouragement in helping me see this through" advises Gez

Everyone gives Mike a standing ovation …
"Harry, for his Instrumentals set" adds Gez (Laughing)

Another standing ovation …

"Can I interest you all in coming to another event?" asks Gez

"Yes" is the enthusiastic response from all members …
"OK, the next event will be … A Tribute to ELVIS" explains Gez (Lots of applause)

"We will have, live on stage, the one and only Rockin' Bobby" advises Gez

"Once again it will be staged here, at CJ's Bar on Saturday, 12th of October ... more details to follow" adds Gez (Laughing)
Everybody is excited to hear of
the new event ...
Gez suddenly brings them all
down to earth ...
"Now, it's time for me and Danny to come amongst you girls" advises Gez
"What are you saying?" laughs Mike

"Don't all fight over us at once" laughs Danny

"Well, you can have my body for
nothing" shouts Danny

Gez looks concerned ...
"Danny, are you feeling
OK?" asks Gez
"Don't forget Ernest"
laughs Mike
"Oh, he's already pulled"
adds Mike
After a few more dances with Carla and Sally, Gez has to go back to the music ...
Ernest asks for a specific record to be played ...
"You can get it if you really want it"
whispers Ernest (Laughing)
"Looks like you already have, mate" says
Mike (Laughing)

"What's he got down his trousers?" asks Mike (Laughing)
"I don't know ... but you can bet it's not sausage meat" laughs Mike
Danny pulls Gez to one side ...
"Hey, Gezza ... those two nurses are giving you the eye" advises Danny (Smiling)
"Well, they've both got excellent taste ... too bad Rick isn't here" replies Gez
"We'd only ban him, anyway" replies Mike
"Tickets are always sold out to him" explains Mike (All Laughing)
"OK, gentlemen ... it's time to change the tempo" advises Gez
"Here's a special mix, everyone" announces Gez
All Zodiac members get back on to the dance floor in droves ...
"How do you do it?" asks Danny
"Oh, I work to a script ... yea, everything is on the list" advises Gez
"It's the easiest way to showcase our talents, Danny" explains Gez
"Besides if a lady comes up to talk to you ... and you find yourself lost, you can just refer to the list, and get back on track ... believe me, it works" advises Gez (Smiling)
"Danny ... we'll do events together, in the future" advises Gez
"Oh, I'm up for that ... your on" replies Danny (Smiling)

Ernest moves across the floor to join Gez and Danny at the DJ console …
"Ernest, are you being a good boy?" asks Gez (Smiling)
"You know me … I have to keep my pecker up" replies Ernest (All Laughing)
"Where are those two nurses?" asks Ernest
"I'm looking for a kind nurse" adds Ernest (Everyone Laughing)

"It looks like you've got your hands full already, Ernest" replies Gez (Smiling)

Carla decides to move across to the DJ console and goes in for the kill …

"Well, are you going to dance with me, or what?" asks Carla (Big Smile)

"OK, honey, your on … by the way do you come here often?" replies Gez (Smiling)
"No, I'm usually up to my neck, at Leeds General Infirmary" replies Carla
"You say the most wonderful things" replies Gez (Smiling)
"I've never been to Leeds General Infirmary" adds Gez
"Maybe one day you will" replies Carla
"Only to see you, love" whispers
Gez (Smiling)
"You a real flatterer, Gez" advises
Carla (Smiling)
Carla goes to find Sally …

216

Danny puts Gez in the picture with regards to Carla …

"You've done very well for yourself, mate" advises Danny (Laughing)

"I'm just being friendly, Danny, just being friendly" explains Gez (Smiling)
"I think she's got the hots for you, Gezza" adds Danny

"Oh, I think Carla's got more than being friends on her mind … she looks to have only got eyes for you, pal" explains Danny (Laughing)
"Take it from me, I know it, when I see it" adds Danny
"Carla's a lovely girl, but …" answers Gez
"Why are you holding back, Gezza?" asks Danny

"I'm not holding back, but right now, I just can't explain anything, OK?" replies Gez
"The other little blonde, Sally, is up for some fun, too" explains Gez (Smiling)
"Go on Daniel, make her day" adds Gez (Laughing)
"What about you, Gezza?" asks Danny

"Oh … once bitten … twice shy … if you get my drift?" advises Gez

"So what about Carla?" asks Danny
"Let's keep it all nice and friendly … then no harm done" explains Gez
"Hey, remember that woman at MIRAGE … Patsy … you know, the club bike?" asks Danny

(Laughing)
"Yea, I remember … oh, no … you didn't?" replies Gez (Laughing)
"Oh yes, I bloody well did" laughs Danny
"Danny … have you no shame?" adds Gez (Laughing)
"Just don't let on to anyone at Mirage, OK?" advises Gez
"Oh, I don't care what they think … it'll give them something to talk about" laughs Danny
"I'm so glad Carla and Sally aren't like that" explains Gez (Smiling)
"Oh, they are all like that … one way or another" laughs Danny
It's almost time for the last dance …
"I have to play the love songs mix … Danny it's time for you to take your pick" advises Gez (Smiling)
The Love songs mix gets under way and Gez makes an announcement …

"OK, sorry everyone, but we've reached the end of the show … it's time for our last boogie" explains Gez (Smiling)
"OK, everyone on the floor for Simply the Best" advises Gez
The floor is suddenly rammed with Zodiac members …
Gez notices Danny is having a whale of a time …

"Danny … put that woman down" advises Gez (Everyone Laughing)

"OK, safe journeys home, everyone … watch out for

our next Event in October" advises Gez (Smiling)
Lots of kissing and smooching is taking place ...

"Come on, love, it's time for you" advises Carla (Big Smile)

"OK, Carla" replies Gez (Smiling)
"Well, did you enjoy your evening?" asks Gez
"Oh, yea, especially with you" beams Carla
Gez looks a little shy, but Carla decides to go in for the kill ...
"Well, are you going to ask me out or what?" asks Carla (Smiling)
"Yea, sure ... when are you off duty?" asks Gez
"I'll let you know, love" replies Carla (Smiling)

"OK, in the meantime, keep everything nice and warm" explains Gez

"Oh, I will, love ... just for you" beams Carla
"Are you going to take me home?" asks Carla

"Yes of course ... just wait till I get everything sorted here" replies Gez

Mike looks the worse for wear ...
"Mike, are you OK?" asks Gez (Looks concerned)
"Oh, I've had one over the eight, Gezza" advises Mike
"OK, don't worry, come home with me and Carla" explains Gez

"Thanks, Gezza, I will" replies Mike
"What are friends for" explains Gez

ZODIAC REVIEW - THE EVENT: A CELEBRATION DISCO

In March, 1991, a review of Gez's first Event at CJ's Bar was in the bulletin ... Thank you for making THE EVENT a brilliant success!
The venue was just right for staging this occasion, and everyone enjoyed the party atmosphere. It really was a night to remember!
We danced to rock n roll, disco music and love songs.

We had a few technical problems with electrical equipment that infiltrated our guest artistes electric guitar, but we managed to sort these out eventually. Thanks to Harry for entertaining us so well with your instrumentals!

The Event was a sell out 3 weeks before the night! I was overwhelmed by it! However, to avoid disappointment, and we speak for other party organisers, it is better to obtain tickets before the night, and not leave it until the last minute!
Special thanks must be extended to Mike, Ernest, Chris and Tony, but especially to Mike for his belief and encouragement in helping me see this through! You may like to know that I'm planning THE EVENT 2 – A TRIBUTE TO ELVIS, complete with a disco. This will be staged in September. More about this in the future. Watch the Events board for more

information!
Finally, my sincere thanks to one and all for coming to my first event ... here's to the next one!
ZODIAC LEEDS are
number one!
See you at a Bar Night,
maybe?
Gez (Leeds Link)

AS ONE DOOR CLOSES … CALLING ELVIS!

Tuesday, Tapas Bar Night … Ernest, Gez and Mike are talking about the Event at CJ's Bar, and the praise is overwhelming …

"Fabulous party, last Saturday, Gezza" advises Ernest (Shaking hands)

"Thanks, Ernest … I hope it's the first of many, and I'm just putting together the next one" replies Gez (Smiling)

"Great … keep me posted, lad" replies Ernest (Smiling)

"Don't worry, Ernest … I promise to let you and Mike know first" adds Gez (Laughing)
Mike arrives, followed by Carla
and Sally …
"Hello, Mike … are you OK?"
asks Gez (Smiling)
"As fit as a butcher's dog,
Gezza" laughs Mike
"Great reviews for your event, mate" explains Mike (Pointing to the bulletin)
"You've put Leeds on the map" adds Mike
"Thanks, Mike … but I really couldn't have done it without your help" replies Gez (Smiles)
"All we did, was encourage you … isn't that right, Ernest?" asks Mike

"Yes, absolutely" replies Ernest
Sally and Carla are in the bar area, and come over to congratulate Gez …
"We loved your party at the weekend" gushes Sally (Big Smile)
"Too bad we didn't have that many dances" advises Carla (Smiling)
"Oh, sorry, duty calls you know, and I couldn't be in two places at the same time

… we'll dance tonight,
OK?" asks Gez

"OK, by me, love" replies
Carla (Smiling)
"Have you checked the Events board?" asks Gez (Smiling)

"There's something on at a venue near Pontefract Race Course, this weekend" explains Gez
"Oh, sorry, love … but I'm working this weekend" advises Carla (Big Smile)
"What about you, Sally?" asks Gez
"Oh, I'll have to check if I'm on or not … I will let you know" replies Sally (Smiles)
"Well, I'll be there with Danny … I hope you can join us" adds Gez
Ernest looks away and laughs to himself …
Carla and Sally retreat to the bar for a refill …

"What are you laughing at, Ernest?" asks
Mike (Looks intrigued)

"Oh, I'm sorry for Gez, he's a nice lad"

replies Ernest

"Why are you sorry, Ernest?" asks Gez (Looks puzzled)

"Oh, you and Florence Nightingale" laughs Ernest

The DJ starts to play various upbeat music.

Gez has a few dances with Carla but that's all that happened!

"Anyhow, I have to arrange to meet Harry about seeing Rocking Bobby perform, and then book him for our do in October" explains Gez

"Will you be there, Mike?" asks Gez

"Yes, and Ernest, too" replies Mike

It's Friday night, lots of Zodiac members arrive at the Pontefract do …

Danny and Gez start to mingle …

"Hi, we're Gez and Danny from Leeds" advises Gez (Smiling)

"Oh Hi, we're Margaret and Bernie … we're from Wakefield" advises Margaret

Margaret is a busty redhead with refined qualities, Bernie is a petite blonde lady …

"Are you both enjoying the evening?" asks Danny (Smiling)

"Well, we would be, if we could find someone to dance with us" laughs Bernie (Smiling)

"Look no further, at your service, dear ladies"

explains Danny (Laughing)

"Danny, your getting rather suave" advises Gez (Smiling)
"Isn't he just" replies Margaret (Laughing)

Mike and Ernest turn up, and both decide to join Danny and Gez …

"Hey up" laughs Mike
"How's it going?" asks Gez

"Still hanging" replies Ernest (Everyone laughing)

"You had a good night, last weekend, Ernest" advises Gez (Laughing)

"Oh, me and the lad were buzzing" replies Ernest (Smiling)
"The lad?" asks Danny (Smiling)

"Oh, don't ask" advises Mike (Laughing)

"Well, we could be in our element tonight" advises Gez (Laughing)

"Go for it" replies Mike
"Have you been OK, Mike?" asks Gez (Looks concerned)
"Yea, I'm good to go" replies Mike (Laughing)
"Have you had any more meetings of the female kind?" asks Ernest
"What about, Rigger Mortis?" laughs Ernest
Rigour Mortis is a term used after a postmortem …
"Who?" asks Danny (Looks

puzzled)
"Ernest's referring to Carla"
explains Gez
"Well, what's happening?"
asks Mike
"Oh, we're just good friends, that's all there is to it" advises Gez
"Anyway I'm OK … too many meetings and temptations … and I'm trying to be good … you know, show a good example" explains Gez
"Oh, take a leaf out of my book, lad … just go for it" laughs Ernest
"It's a lovely venue, and a pleasure to be here" informs Mike
"Have you been looking into your next do, Gezza?" asks Mike
"Oh, I'm meeting Harry, remember he played instrumentals for us at CJ's?" asks Gez
"Oh, yea … we remember, the guy with the dodgy equipment" replies Mike
"Mine's good to go" laughs Ernest
"Thanks for that, Ernest" laughs Gez

"Anyway, Harry is going to take me to a venue where Rocking Bobby performs … so I'll see him in action, so to speak" advises Gez (Laughing)
"Will you book him there and then?" asks Mike (Looks intrigued)

"Yea, I'll watch his performance and then book him for the October event" replies Gez (Smiling)
"In the meantime, lets get on the dance

floor" advises Mike
"Any ladies, want to join us?" asks Mike (Laughing)
"Oh, yea, we'll join you" replies a voice

"Wow … now don't all rush at once" adds Danny (Laughing)

"It's a stampede" laughs Ernest
"Well, they've all got fabulous taste" replies Gez (Laughing)
"What do you think, Ernest?" asks Gez
"Oh, I agree … the lad's raring to go" quips Ernest (Laughing)
"Down boy, down" replies Jenny (Laughing)
Jenny is a brunette, has brown eyes and a figure to match …
"How does he do it?" asks Danny (Laughing)

"Sheer magnetism … sheer magnetism" replies Ernest (Laughing)

The DJ decides to play a 60s mix …

"Come on, it's back to the Sixties" advises Mike (Laughing)

"The old flower power" replies Gez (Smiling)
The following Wednesday, Gez meets Harry at a pub in Pudsey …
"Hello Harry" advises Gez
"Hi Gez, I'm glad you could make it" replies Harry

"Quick, take a seat, Bobby is about to begin" explains

Harry (Looks excited)

A sudden announcement is made over the microphone ...

"Hi ... it's showtime ... here is the one and only Rocking Bobby" advises the announcer
The pub is packed, and Rocking Bobby is greeted with lots of applause ... Bobby rocks into his set of classic Elvis songs ... everyone is mesmerised by his performance ...
"I have to book him, Harry" advises Gez

"He's got a loyal following and rock and roll dancers too" explains Harry

"Fabulous ... it will be great for my October event" replies Gez (Looks excited)
"I can already visualise the event, Harry" explains Gez

"Harry introduce me to Bobby ... I need to book him" replies Gez (Smiling)

Booby finishes his set and then comes across to join Harry and Gez ...
In pure Elvis drawl he responds ...

"Pleased to meet you partner"
advises Bobby (Smiling)

"Hey, are you free in October?" asks Gez
"Why?" replies Bobby
"Oh, I'm doing an event, and you'll be the star of the show" explains Gez

Booby checks his diary with his daughter. He confirms that he is available on Saturday 12th October.
"Oh, that's great … I'm over the moon, Bobby" advises Gez (Laughing)

"My pleasure … the Rock and Roll dancers will put on a show for us too" adds Bobby
Well, I can tell you … Gez was in wonderland!

"That's fab, Bobby … I'll book the venue and advise you, if that's OK?" replies Bobby
"OK, by me … Gez" adds Bobby

Gez rebooked CJ's for Saturday 12th October and advertised the Event in the Zodiac magazine … tickets sold like hot cakes.
It was advertised as THE EVENT 2 – A TRIBUTE TO ELVIS. Gez also advised that he would put on a disco to accompany the Event and that Bobby would perform in three sets.
It was perfectly advertised and put on the Events board at Tapas and other Zodiac venues!
It became another SELL OUT, and tickets were only £2 each for a magical night of entertainment.
At the next Bar night in Tapas, Leeds … Mike, Danny and Ernest are looking forward to the coming event …
"Oh, I'm really looking forward to it, Gez"
advises Danny (Smiling)
"I just hope we can pull it off" replies Gez
(Looks concerned)

"Don't worry … you'll do it" assures Mike
"Are there many girls going?" asks Ernest (Laughing)
"More than you can handle" adds
Mike (Laughing)
"Oh, I'm up for that" quips Ernest
"I'll dig out my old Teddy Boy suit"
adds Ernest (Laughing)
"Now that we must see" replies Mike
(All Laughing)
It's the night everyone has been waiting for … CJ's Bar … THE EVENT 2 – A TRIBUTE TO ELVIS … The stage is set, the atmosphere is electrifying … then suddenly the show is rolling …
"Are you ready for tonight, Bobby?" asks Gez (Looks excited)

"Oh, I'm in good voice tonight … I can't wait to get rocking" enthuses Bobby

Mike comes over to talk to Gez …
"The place is buzzing tonight, Mike"
advises Gez (Smiling)
"Yea … you've done us all proud, again"
explains Mike (Looks happy)
"It's going to be a night to remember" adds Mike (Laughing)

Bobby gets ready for his performance …

"Hi, everyone … welcome to our Tribute to Elvis night" advises Gez

Lots of applause … the place is really buzzing …

"I'm ready … Rocking Bobby is ready … are you ready?" asks Gez
"We've got the music … have you all got the passion?" adds Gez
Everyone shouts a resounding "Yes"
Gez plays the Elvis
intro music … Also
Sprach Zarathustra …
Bobby, suddenly enters to rapturous applause …

Bobby belts out a string of Elvis hits … everyone's excited by his show … The Rock n Roll dancers accompany Bobby …
"Fabulous night" advises
Danny (Smiling)
"You've done it" adds Mike
(Laughing)
Both shake hands with Gez …

"You've got legendary Zodiac status" explains Mike

"I couldn't have done it without both of you" advises Gez

"It takes me back to my quiff, and winkle picker days" advises Ernest (Laughing)

"Love the Teddy Boy outfit, Ernest" advises Gez (Laughing)
"So, do the ladies … thanks, lad" replies
Ernest (Laughing)
"Great night" quips Danny
"I'm so happy when I hear just how much our members have enjoyed themselves" advises Gez

(Smiling)
"This is, without saying, the most gratifying statement of all, and well it spurs me on, to better things" explains Gez (Looks excited)
Rocking Bobby takes to the stage again, this time he is dressed in a full white Elvis type jump suit ...
"Oh, the place is jumping ... come on let's all rock" quips Bobby
Ernest takes to the floor ...
"Remember your dicky heart, Ernest" advises Mike (Looks concerned)
"Oh, I'm OK ... got to keep the lad happy" laughs Ernest
Ernest becomes surrounded by a bevy of women ...
"How does he do it?" asks Danny (Looks stunned)
"He's just a magnet, I guess" replies Gez (Laughing)
"Who's that with him?" asks Danny
"Hey, he's got my woman ... saucy old man" laughs Danny
"Don't worry, she'll be back" advises Mike
It's smooch time and the end of the night ...
Suddenly, Gez makes an announcement ...
"I'm thinking of planning another event ... are you all up for it?" asks Gez

Everyone shouts "Yes"

"I'm planning THE EVENT 3 – A CHRISTMAS DISCO with Live on Stage ... Davy Johnson ... a country and western artiste" explains Gez (Lots of applause)

"I hope your not all superstitious, though ... it'll be on Friday 13th December?" asks Gez

Everyone agrees it will be another wonderful event, just before Christmas.

"Oh, it's not my lucky number" advises Ernest (Looks shocked)

"Are you up for it, Mike?" asks Gez

"Absolutely, Gezza ... you can count me in" replies Mike (Laughing)

"Danny is already primed" advises Gez

"Hey, I can be Santa, again" advises Ernest (Laughing)

"I'll get all those girls sat on my knee" adds Ernest (Full of glee)

"You'll have to be a good boy, Ernest" advises Mike

"Get down, shep" replies Ernest (Laughing)

"We need to set a trend, Gezza" advises Mike

"A trend?" asks Gez (Looks puzzled)

"Yea, a gimmick" replies Mike (Smiling)

"I've got it ... we can ask all the Zodiac members to wear something red for Christmas" replies Gez

"Yes, that's it, simple but effective"
advises Mike (Laughing)
"It should prove to be another sell out,
Mike" replies Gez
"OK, we can start to sell our tickets at the next
bar night" advises Gez
"We're all with you" advises Danny
As predicted, it was yet another SOLD OUT Event,
weeks before it was due to take place!
This time with a difference …

Mike, Ernest and Gez in conversation at the next Tapas Bar night …

"So, Gezza what's on the agenda for the Christmas do?" asks Mike (Looks intrigued)

"Well, Mike I've had an idea" replies Gez
"Go, on" asks Mike (Looks puzzled)

"I'm planning a stage version of an old show … Christmas Blind Date at CJ's … what do you think?" asks Gez
"Oh, I'm up for that"
advises Ernest
"Your up for anything"
laughs Mike
"We'll put you in reserve, OK?"
adds Mike
"What do you think, Danny?"
asks Gez (Smiling)
"I think it's a good idea, Gezza" replies
Danny (Laughing)

"How will it work?" asks Mike (Still looks puzzled)
"We'll ask for three guys and three girls to be contestants … and one guy and one girl as pickers" explains Gez
"Sounds good to me"
replies Mike
"I'll host it" explains
Gez (Smiles)
"We'll give a prize to the winning couple and a contribution towards a date of their choice, with a bottle of bubbly for the runners up" advises Gez
"Sounds like another memorable night"
replies Mike (Smiling)
"It's another Zodiac Leeds, first" explains
Mike
"It's sure to be sold out in a few weeks, tickets are on sale now" adds Gez

"As long as there will be plenty of ladies, then I'm happy" adds Ernest (Laughing)

"Don't worry, Ernest, you'll be well catered for" laughs Danny

"As long as you behave yourself, Ernest … don't let us down" replies Mike

"You know me, I'm the soul of discretion" advises Ernest (Smiling)

"That's what we're worried about, Ernest" explains Mike
"It's OK … scouts honour" quips Ernest (Laughing)
"OK, Ernest … you've convinced us" replies Gez
"What do you think, Mike?" asks Gez (Smiling)
"I think it'll be another great night, Gezza" replies Mike (Laughing)
"Where's the brunette and the bubbly blonde, tonight?" asks Mike
"Oh, do you mean Carla and Sally?" replies Gez
The door to Tapas opens … Carla and Sally enter and head towards Mike and Gez …
"Hi" beams Carla

"Have we missed anything?" asks Sally (Smiling)

"Not really … we're just talking about the Christmas Event" replies Gez (Smiling)

"You are going to be there, aren't you Carla?" asks Gez

"Oh, yes I'll be there, love" replies Carla (Beaming)

"How about you, Sally?" asks Mike

"Oh, I'm coming, love … it looks like the event of the year" replies Sally

"Well, it will be fun, that's for sure" explains Gez

"Are we your favourite girls?" asks Carla

"Your my favourite nurses, that's for sure" quips Gez

ZODIAC REVIEW – CALLING ELVIS ... AND THE EVENT 3 – CHRISTMAS DISCO

The stage was set, the atmosphere was electrifying ... then suddenly THE EVENT was rolling, and Rocking Bobby, took centre stage.

It was the start of another special night to remember!

In fact the reception from the very start was tremendous.

I know, Bobby was overwhelmed by the response he received, and was on top singing form all evening. His first set went down extremely well. We all knew we were in for a good night!

When Bobby appeared in his special "Tribute to Elvis" the reception from all Zodiac members was fantastic.

It was a great night, and the response from Zodiac members was well received. It was an exciting evening from beginning to end and we had added entertainment from the Rock n Roll dancers, weren't they good?

As a follow up, tickets will be on sale for Event 3 – Christmas Disco, again at CJ's on Friday 13th December!

The feedback received for the first two events has been very gratifying.

Tickets were SOLD OUT well in advance. It seems we're getting a reputation for putting on a good show in Leeds!
Thank you everyone for making THE EVENT such a brilliant success! See you at the Christmas Disco or Bar night, maybe!

Keep on
Rocking

Gez

A SQUARE PEG IN A ROUND HOLE/CHRISTMAS EVENT

After another sure fire sell out of tickets for the Christmas disco at CJ's, the night eventually arrives, on the back of two previously successful events ...
Mike and Gez are in conversation at
Tapas Bar night in Leeds ...
"It's been another exciting sell out, Mike"
advises Gez
"You've built up a real following now ... everyone has only good things to say about you" replies Mike (Smiling)
"Wow ... I'm so flattered, Mike"
advises Gez (Blushing)
"I've got things to follow up next
year" adds Gez
"My, your thinking far ahead" replies Mike (Smiling)
"What have you got in mind?" asks Mike (Looks puzzled)
"Well, I'm thinking of taking part in the ITV TELETHON 92" explains Gez (Looks excited)
"Wow, you are thinking big, Gezza" advises Mike
"The actual on the day event is being staged at Harewood House" adds Gez (Still excited)
"What do you think, Mike?" asks Gez (Smiling)
"It sounds exciting ... it'll be the making of you" replies Mike (Laughing)

"You'll have legendary status at Zodiac … if that happens" explains Mike
"We'll all back you up, Gezza" adds Mike
"… but let's get through tonight, first, Gezza" laughs Mike

The following Friday, CJ'S Bar, THE EVENT 3 – CHRISTMAS DISCO …

Mike and Gez are already at the venue, and setting up the disco equipment … Zodiac members start to arrive at the event, which is taking place on the first floor party area.
Gez, suddenly takes to the microphone …
"We'd like to welcome you all to CJ's for our Christmas Event" advises Gez (Smiling)

"We have Davy Johnson live on stage in 45 minutes plus a very special Christmas version of Blind Date between 9.30 and 10pm" explains Gez (Smiling)
"You all look amazing in your Christmas gear … there's tinsel everywhere … most of it is on Ernest" advises Gez (Everyone Laughing)
"OK, let's see you all on the dance floor, here's our special Christmas mix" adds Gez (Points to dance floor)
Danny takes over the DJ spot for a while …

Gez decides to circulate and talks to a lot of Zodiac members, meeting Kris from Wakefield for the first time …
"Hi, I'm Kris, from Wakefield … this is Stella" advises a voice (Big Smile)
Carla and Sally arrive at the venue …

Carla is five foot seven, has long brown hair, and very attractive. Sally is five foot six, has blonde curly hair … both are single and in their early thirties … …
"Hi, Kris … I'm Gez" (Smiles)

"Oh, I know love … everyone seems to know you, here" replies Kris (Smiling)

"Oh, they do?" asks Gez (Still smiling)
"My reputation precedes me"
laughs Gez
Ernest joins Gez and Kris …
"Ernest, look at you" laughs Gez

"Well, it's Christmas …and you did say, dress for the occasion" explains Ernest (Laughing)
"Kris, this is Ernest … he's a Zodiac phenomenon" advises Gez (Smiling)
"Hi, I'm Kris" beams Kris
"You know our Gezza, has got all the girls following him" advises Ernest (Smiling)
"Oh, he's exaggerating, Kris" replies Gez (Smiling)
"No … he really has" explains Ernest (Laughs)

"What can I say" replies Gez
(Looking embarrassed)

"Is it your first event, Kris?" asks
Gez
"Yes, first of many, I hope" advises Kris (Big Smile)

"I'm so glad you made it to our Christmas event … your both going to love it at Zodiac … we have lots on the horizon for next year" advises Gez (Smiling)

"We'll have a dance later, Kris ... must get back to the music and let Danny free" explains Gez
"OK, love ... I'll hold you to that" beams Kris

"I'll be back ... keep everything nice and warm" adds Gez (Smiling)

"Oh, I will love ... I will" laughs Kris
"Your in there" advises
Ernest (Laughing)
"Oh, stop it, Ernest" laughs
Gez
Gez makes an announcement ...

"OK, it's time for Davy Johnson ... live on stage" advises Gez

The dance floor clears, and Davy begins his set ...
Mike comes across to Gez ...

"I'm not keen on him, Gezza" advises Mike (Looks very concerned)

"No, I agree" advises Danny (Looks subdued)
Davy was a shadow of Rocking Bobby and at best, a club turn!
We cut short his set ...

"Thanks Davy, brilliant set ... but it's almost time for our Christmas Blind Date ...with a difference" announces Gez (Smiling)
"You cut Davy short, rather quickly" advises Danny

"We had to, Danny ... the place was dying" explains Gez

"There was no atmosphere, it was dead" adds Mike

"Anyway, we're back on track, now" adds Gez (Smiling)

"Right, can I have those taking part to the stage please?" asks Gez (Smiling)

"Who's hosting it?" asks Ernest (Laughing)

"Guess" replies Gez (Laughing)

"Well, you can't have everything" laughs Ernest

"Well OK, Ernest in your case you can" replies Gez (Laughing)

"OK in this version our Pickers will be blind folded and the 3 boy and 3 girl contestants will sit on chairs on the stage" explains Gez (Points to dance floor)

"Are you with me, so far?" asks Gez (Smiling)

"Oh, yes" shout all members (Laughing)

Gez plays the Blind Date theme and begins to whip up the crowd of Zodiac members ...

"OK, number one ... what's your name and where do you come from?" asks Gez

"Hi, I'm Sandy, and I'm from Leeds" advises contestant number one (Lots of applause)

"Hello, Sandy ... what are you looking for in a man?" asks Gez (Smiling)

"Oh, he must be fairly good looking, like you, love … and clever too" advises Sandy (Everyone Laughing)
"Oh, thanks … we'll see if we can oblige" replies Gez (Looking embarrassed)
And so, it went on and on … it was all done in good taste with a sense of fun. It made the evening!
We successfully paired off a two couples, and gave them a contribution to a date of their choice … the runners up were given a bottle of bubbly … it was another roaring success!
Gez planned a follow up event in March!

"I'll be in the next one" advises Ernest (Laughing)

"OK, we'll book your place, now, Ernest" laughs Mike
"I can show them all my virtuosity" explains Ernest (Everyone Laughing)
"Whatever does he mean?" asks Kris (Smiling)
"We're not really sure, Ernest talks in riddles" laughs Mike
Another Christmas mix is now being played by Danny …
Everyone was, well and truly, in the Christmas spirit … and they all loved it! Danny continues to be DJ, while Gez mingles …
Gez dances with Kris for a while …

"So, Kris, what are you looking for?" asks Gez (Smiling)

"Oh, I'm just here to have fun … I'm not into bodies" explains Kris (Smiling)

"Oh, I understand what you mean … once you venture down that road, who knows?" replies Gez (Looks pensive)
"What about you?" asks Kris

"I'm just window shopping … but I'm like a square peg in a round hole" explains Gez
"What do you mean, love?" asks Kris (Looks intrigued)

"All I want is to have some fun … but there are those who are looking for a permanent one … know what I mean?" asks Gez
"They just don't understand if you tell them … I'm only here for fun" adds Gez
"Anyway, life's too complicated" explains Gez (Smiling)
"Oh, I'm the same … I agree, love" replies Kris

"Before you know it … the wedding bells are ringing" adds Kris

"Are you up for that, Kris?" asks Gez
"You must be joking" laughs Kris

"Your right I am joking … I just wanted to see your reaction" explains Gez

"It was priceless" laughs Gez
"What about you?" asks Kris (Smiling)

"What about me?" replies Gez

"Well, have you ever been married, love?" asks Kris

"Oh, no ... I'm a bachelor" explains Gez (Smiling)

"Are you a confirmed bachelor?" asks Kris

"Oh, no ... I don't think so ... but like I said before, life's complicated" adds Gez (Now on his guard)

"In what way?" asks Kris (Looks intrigued)

"Oh, it just is ... that's it" replies Gez (Smiling)

"I'm so glad, we're both on the same wavelength" adds Kris (Smiling)

"I'd probably run a mile, anyway" advises Gez

"Some are hooked, before they know it" adds Gez

"Just set out your stall from the start, that's what I think" explains Kris (Smiling)

"What about friends with benefits?" asks Kris

"It depends what you mean by that?" asks Gez (Looks surprised)

"Oh, you know" advises Kris (Winks)

"I guess I do" replies Gez

"Well?" asks Kris

"Well, maybe" replies Gez

"I'd better get back to Danny, and take over for a

while, Kris" advises Gez

"You'll like Danny, he's on the same wavelength as us" explains Gez (Smiling)
"OK … hey, where's my Christmas kiss?" asks Kris (Smiling)
"Here's a smacker to be going on with" adds Kris
"Come back for more" advises Kris (Big Smile)

"Oh, I will Kris, I will … your naughty" replies Gez (Smiling)

"Do you like naughty" asks Kris (Laughs)
"Oh, I love it" replies Gez (Smiling)

Danny steps down from the DJ console and Gez takes over …

An announcement is made by Gez …
"Well, we've almost come to the end of the night" advises Gez (Looks sad)

"Let's see you all on the dance floor for the Zodiac anthem … SIMPLY THE BEST by TINA TURNER" explains Gez
The dance floor fills to almost capacity …

"On behalf of Zodiac may we wish you all a very happy Christmas … we'll see you at some of the events over Christmas or at Tapas … now it's time for a smooch" advises Gez (Smiles)

Kris comes over to Gez at the DJ console …
"Hey, do you want a smooch with

me?" asks Kris (Smiling)
"I thought you'd never ask, love" replies Gez (Smiling)
"Well, sometimes I have a need … don't you?" asks Kris (Looks mischievous)
"Oh, yes, obviously" adds Gez (Smiling)
"Maybe, we can help each other out" asks Kris
"Oh, I'd love to" replies Gez (Looks surprised)
"Come round on Christmas day, OK?" asks Kris (Smiling)

Ernest moves across the floor to speak to Gez …

"I've had a good night, tonight" advises Ernest

"Did you?" asks Gez
"Oh, yea … I scored with that little blonde" replies Ernest (Smiling)
"OK, what's she called then?" asks Mike (Smiling)
"She's call Laura" advises Ernest

"Ernest, I don't know how you do it?" advises Mike (Laughing)

"Sheer magnetism, Mike … sheer magnetism" explains Ernest (Laughing)

"If you've got it … flaunt it" adds Ernest (Smiling)

"Exactly" replies Mike (Laughing)

"Mike, how did you get on?" asks Gez (Smiling)

"Oh, Wanda was in tonight" replies Mike

"I thought you weren't going to …" asks Gez

"Oh, it's Christmas … and time to pull the cracker" laughs Mike

"Pull his plonker, more like" laughs Ernest

"Anyhow, you don't seem to be doing too bad either, Gezza" advises Mike (Smiling)

"Oh, we're just good friends, Kris is new tonight" replies Gez (Smiling)

"I've heard that one before" laughs Ernest

"Where's the little blonde and brunette, tonight?" asks Mike

"Oh, you mean … Sally and Carla?" asks Gez (Smiling)

"Yea, obviously" replies Mike

"They must both be on duty" replies Gez

"Are they cops?" asks Ernest (Laughing)

"No … they both work at Leeds General Infirmary" replies Gez (Smiling)

"Doctors?" asks Ernest

"They are both nurses" explains Gez (Laughing)

"Well, they have both got the hots for you lad" advises Ernest

"How do you know?" asks Gez (Looks surprised)

"Oh, I can see it in their eyes" replies Ernest

"You can take your pick there" explains Ernest (Smiling)

YOU CAN GET IT IF YOU REALLY WANT IT!

Tuesday Bar night, Tapas, Lower Briggate, Leeds ... Mike, Danny, Gez and Ernest are in conversation in

the bar area …
"You can get it, if you really want it" advises Ernest (Laughing)
"Guaranteed" replies Mike (Laughing)
"Motion carried" replies Ernest (Laughing)
"I'll second that" replies Danny (Smiling)
"Well, you seemed to be having a good time at your Christmas event last Friday?" asks Ernest (Smiling)
"Oh, I was … Kris is a lovely lady" advises Gez (Smiling)

"No ifs, no buts … you should have gone for it" advises Ernest

"I'd have filled my boots there" replies Mike (Laughing)
"… and I'm going to try that one next time" adds Mike

As Tapas starts to fill up with Zodiac members, Sally enters … alone …

"Where's Carla?" asks Gez (Looks around)
"Oh, she's decided not to come any more, for some reason" advises Sally
"I hope that reason wasn't because of me" replies Gez
"Well …" replies Sally

"It is about me … oh, I'm so sorry" explains Gez (Looks sad)

"You should have asked her out" advises Mike (Looks serious)
"Oh, yea ... maybe I should ... I liked Carla" replies Gez
"It's never too late" replies Ernest
"We'll see" replies Gez

Gez talks to Sally and advises that he is unhappy about Carla ...
"I saw you with Dave last week, Sally ... what's happened to him?" asks Gez (Looks concerned)
"Oh, he just dumped me" advises Sally (Tearful)
"And you being so attractive" replies Ernest (Looking concerned)
"Why did he dump you, Sally?" asks Gez (Very concerned)
Sally is very tearful but holds back her tears ...
"I don't know, he just did" explains Sally
Gez puts his arm around Sally and reassures her ...

"I'm so sorry to hear that, don't worry there's plenty of more fish in the sea" advises Gez (Smiling)
"Yea, there's as good a fish in the sea that ever came out of it" quips Ernest
Sally goes off to powder her nose ...
"She's a pretty girl, it won't be long before she's snapped up" advises Ernest
"Don't you fancy her?" asks Mike (Smiling)
"Yes, of course I do" replies Gez (Smiling)

Sally returns back down stairs ...
The DJ begins to play 80s anthems ...

"Come on, Sally ... let's get on the dance floor, love" asks Gez (Smiling)

After a few dances ... Gez asks Sally for a kiss ...

"Well, are you going to kiss me, or what?" asks Gez (Smiling)

Sally obviously obliged ... and it wasn't just a peck on the cheek ... it was a real smacker!
"Do you fancy going to Pudsey Civic at the weekend?" asks Sally (Smiling)
"Yes, I'd love to go with you" replies Gez (Smiling)
"OK, here's my phone number ... call me on Thursday, then I'll know if I'm working or not then" explains Sally
"OK, Sally ... yea I promise to phone you" replies Gez

But it never happened ... Sally had to work shifts and Gez eventually saw her with Jack, but she always seemed to carry a torch for him!
Jack is in his late fifties. Almost 20 years or more older than Sally ...

At another Tapas Bar night ... Ernest is as always, the soul of discretion?

"Well, you lost out there, big time, lad" advises Ernest
"What do you mean, Ernest?" asks Gez
(Looking puzzled)
"That Sally ... you know" laughs Ernest

"Thanks for the advice, Ernest" replies Gez

"Why do nice girls always go for somebody like that?" asks Gez (Looks concerned)

"It's an age old question, lad" explains Ernest
"Well. what's your take on it, Ernest?" asks Gez
"Money lad, money ... money talks" laughs Ernest
"Anyway it's perhaps for the best" explains Gez
"What do you mean, lad?" asks Ernest
"Just take my word for it, Ernest" adds Gez

It was obvious, Jack and Sally, had become an item!

Everyone questioned why they still came to Zodiac, as a couple? It all seemed a bit strange, but that's the magic of it all, maybe? "You can get it if you really want it, lad" quips Ernest (Laughing)

"I'll leave that to you, Ernest" replies Gez
Kris arrives at Tapas, and Gez decides to join her at the bar ...
Gez warns Kris of a possible invite by Ernest ...
"Oh, don't worry, Gez ... he's got no chance ... while you have every chance" replies Kris (Smiling)
"Sometimes having no words ... say

everything" replies Gez (Smiling)
"You always say the loveliest things" explains Kris
"I've got my little outfit for Christmas day, love" explains Kris (Smiling)
"Oh, it sounds good, Kris" replies Gez (Smiling)
"Oh, you'll love it … it's so tiny" advises Kris (Big Smile)
"Wow" adds Gez (Looks stunned)
"Well, that's what friends with benefits, are for" laughs Kris

"Have you any special requests for on the day?" asks Kris (Smiling)

"Later, love" replies Gez (Smiling)
"Is there anything on, at the weekend?" asks Kris

"Well, there's an event in Pudsey, at someone's house" replies Gez

"OK, lets go to it, love" answers Kris
A new member to join Zodiac was Robert …
"Hi, I'm Robert" advises a voice
Robert is 6ft tall, balding, has brown eyes and has a positive way about him …
"Hi, I'm Gez … I'm one of the organisers with Mike at Leeds" advises Gez (Both shake hands)
"OK, go and check out our Events board … there's

something on at Pudsey at the weekend" explains Gez
"See you there" replies Robert (Smiling)

The weekend arrives and it's a first time party for 2 girls ... but there are major problems ...
A punch up almost takes place concerning Zodiac members and gate crashers!

Gez has to intervene to bring the situation under control ...

"Robert, don't get involved, mate" advises Gez
"We'll deal with it internally" explains Gez
"Zodiac don't need this at any of our events" adds Gez (Looks anxious)
"Are you OK, Robert?" asks Gez (Looking concerned)
"Yea, I'm OK, Gez" advises Robert
"We'll inform David ... their memberships will be cancelled" explains Gez

Gladly, Robert took our advice, and Zodiac excluded the 2 women members due to a high tension situation.
Robert went on to be a good friend of Gez ... he called himself "Best Pal" and he liked to be known by this at Bar nights and Events!
Robert, blossomed at Zodiac, and he eventually put on a real show of strength with our Truck Pull Challenge at Harewood House the following year!
Those were Zodiac's golden years!

At another Zodiac Christmas Party at the Queens Hotel in Leeds, members gathered for our annual dinner dance in the private Ballroom …

The resident DJ played various pop songs and all the Christmas hits …

"This is a very posh venue, Gezza" advises Mike

"Oh, it's the poshest in Leeds, Mike" advises Gez

Ernest joins in the conversation …

"Are you on your best behaviour tonight, Ernest?" asks Mike (Smiling)

"Naturally … I'm always good … it's the others" laughs Ernest

"Oh, they bring out the worst in you, then?" asks Gez (Smiling)

"You got it in one, lad" laughs Ernest

The waitresses begin to serve dinner. Zodiac has over 300 members attending this event.

Everything runs smoothly, and David, the Zodiac Co-ordinator is also in attendance …

A member called Phil was a rather unusual sight …

"I'm determined to get on that dance floor with Annie" advises Phil

"What happened to your foot?" asks David (Looks concerned)

"Oh, it's broken and in a pot … but I'm still here" quips Phil

"Good on you, Phil" replies Mike

(Smiling)
A new member, Pat, had just joined Zodiac … He was blown away on the first night …
"I told you, Pat, that you would be spoilt for choice" advises Gez (Smiling)
"Your a man of your word" laughs Pat
At that point, Jack and Sally arrive, and begin to join in all the festivities!

Gez notices that Sally is secretly watching him …

"Pat, do me a favour, will you?" asks Gez (Smiling)

"What is it, first?" replies Pat (Laughing)
"You see that girl over there?" asks Gez
"The bubble haired blonde?" explains Gez
"Yea, I see her" replies Pat
"Pat, just watch her … is she watching me or what?" asks Gez (Smiling)
"See what you think, and then let me know" explains Gez (Looks concerned)
Kris arrives in the ballroom …

"Hey, what about me?" asks Kris (Smiling)

"Oh, hello, Kris … you look stunning tonight" replies Gez (Smiling)

"I thought you'd like it" replies Kris
"Have you had any more thoughts about,

Christmas day?" asks Kris

"Well, only of you in your tiny outfit" laughs Gez

"Oh, nothing will be left to the imagination, love" explains Kris

"Have you any requests, for under wear?" asks Kris (Winks)

Gez is completely taken by surprise at this question ...

"Black ... wear black" replies Gez (Smiling)

"OK, love ... you'll not be disappointed" explains Kris

Pat returns to talk to Gez ...

"Well, Pat ... what have you found out?" asks Gez

"She hasn't taken her eyes off you, all night, mate" advises Pat

"I just don't understand it, do you?" replies Gez (Looks stunned)

"If I was with someone they would be the only ones I'd have eyes for" explains Gez

"Well, you can take it from me, she can't take her eyes off you" adds Pat

"Well, it's too late now" replies Gez

It was another fabulous night ... the atmosphere and occasion made it!

Next up, it's Christmas day ... and Gez arrives at Kris's house in Wakefield ... Gez knocks on the door ...

Kris arrives at the door, wearing a

raincoat … only a raincoat!
Gez enters and Kris opens her raincoat …
"Wow, Kris you look stunning" advises Gez (Smiling)
"I thought you'd love my tiny outfit" replies Kris (Smiling)

"I'm wearing stockings and suspenders, just for you" adds Kris (Looks sexy)

"I think I'm going to enjoy friends with benefits" replies Gez (Smiling)
"Me, too" adds Kris (Smiles)

It's the Tuesday Bar night at Tapas in between Christmas and New Year's Eve … Mike and Gez are in conversation near the bar area …
"I'm glad to see that your enjoying yourself more, Gezza" advises Mike
"Oh, I'm starting to unwind a bit now, Mike" replies Gez
"Are you going to the New Year's Eve party, Mike?" asks Gez
"Try and stop me, I'll be there,
mate" replies Mike
Pat and Danny arrive at Tapas …
"Pat are you planning on coming to the New Year's Eve party?" asks Gez
"Yea, I'll be there" advises Pat
"It'll be fun all the way … Danny's coming too" explains Pat
"It's going to be a fabulous end to the year" replies Mike (All Laughing)

A WORD IN YOUR SHELL LIKE!

Mike and Gez are summoned to see David at his office in Leeds … Sally returns to Tapas with Carla … a tricky situation … Ernest is at his usual best! Leeds city centre, early evening, Tuesday, 2 hours before Bar Night at Tapas … Zodiac Regional Office. Mike and Gez meet outside the office, which is just situated off Briggate …
"What's it all about, Mike?" asks Gez (Looks puzzled)
"We've been summoned by David" replies Mike (Looks concerned)
"Summoned … I don't get it?" replies Gez
"Oh, don't worry, Gezza … it's nothing we've done" explains Mike

Gez and Mike enter the building. They both make their way into the suite of offices and walk up the ramshackled winding staircase …
"This takes me back, Mike" advises Gez (Smiling)

"Yea, it's almost as if we've entered a time warp" replies Mike (Laughing)

Gez and Mike reach David's office on the second floor …
Both enter to find David on the phone …

"Come in … come in" advises
David (Smiling)
"Sorry I won't be long"
explains David

Gez and Mike sit themselves down in the quaint office surroundings, which is adorned with lots of Zodiac paraphernalia …

David completes his conversation and puts down the phone …

"Another potential member?" asks Mike (Smiling)

"Yes, and another satisfied one too" laughs David

"First time at Zodiac Regional Office for you Gez?" asks David

"Yea, but I'm glad to see where everything begins" replies Gez (Smiling)

"David keeps everything together" advises Mike

"So, I suppose your both wondering why I summoned you to come here tonight?" asks David

"Yea, you could say that, David" replies Mike

"Don't worry it's nothing to do with anything about you" explains David

"That's a relief" laughs Mike

"Members only have good things to say about both of you" advises David

"You've put Leeds on the map, Gez" explains David

"So, what's it all about, David?" asks Mike (Looks puzzled)

"Well, a couple of matters, really" adds David

"Go on, David, tell us all about it" replies Mike

"Right, well I won't beat about the bush ... we've had complaints from several members" advises David (Looks serious)

"What about?" asks Mike (Looks puzzled)

"Well, one of them has decided not to go to Tapas again" replies David (Looks concerned)

"Why, what's happened, David?" asks Gez (Looks puzzled)

"Well, it's because of the embarrassment and humiliation caused by one particular member" explains David

"Embarrassed by whom, David?" asks Gez

"Well, it's been caused by a lady called, Carla" replies David

"Carla ... the nurse?" asks Mike (Looks stunned)

"Yes, I believe she is a nurse" explains David

"Just what is she being accused of?" asks Gez (Looks equally stunned)

"Yea, what's the embarrassment?" asks Mike

"Will this particular member, who shall remain anonymous, says Carla humiliated her in front of lots of other Zodiac members" explains David (Looks anxious)

"Humiliated?" asks Gez (Looks really concerned)

"Yes, apparently Carla was taking the mickey, and calling them names" adds David (Looks mad)
"Wow, I can't believe that Carla would do that" replies Gez (Still stunned)
"Well, it's all true, I'm afraid" replies David
"There are also several witnesses who saw it" explains David
"So, is it the usual penalty, David?" asks Mike
"Yes, I'm afraid so"
replies David
"OK, consider it done"
advises Mike
"We'll do it as soon as possible" advises Mike

"OK, I'm sorry to leave it in your capable hands" replies David

David has a rethink then gives another answer …
"Tell you what"
advises David
"What?" asks Mike
"I'll call into Tapas with you tonight" advises David
"Good idea" replies Gez (Still stunned)
"Why?" asks Mike (Looks concerned)

"Well, maybe on the off chance that Carla may be in tonight" replies David

"If she does turn up … I'll instigate it" adds David

"OK, David, we'd appreciate that" replies Mike "
"… and the other matter?" asks Gez (Looks serious)
"Oh, just to advise you, before you hear it on the grapevine" replies David
"I've stood down, Diane at Harrogate Bar Night" advises David
"Why, what's happened?" asks Mike (Looks concerned)

"Oh, she is no longer the Meet and Greeter there" explains David

"Why, what did she do?" asks Mike (stunned)
"She was running everything, as if she owned it, on her own" advises David (Looks serious)
"We've had lots of complaints about her handling of the Bar night and events" explains David
"That explains why members at Harrogate were never at any of my events" advises Gez (Looks sad)
"Well, it was highly unlikely that your event or any other events outside of Harrogate were publicised at all" explains David (Looks anxious)
"So, who's running it now?" asks Mike

"Someone called, Barry, has taken over the reins" advises David

"Diane is barred, as is Carla" adds David

(Looks serious)

It's nearing 8pm, David, Mike and Gez leave Zodiac Regional Offices and make their way on foot to Tapas in Lower Briggate …

All are greeted on entry by, Bob, the owner …

"Good evening" greets Bob

(Looks happy)

"You all had me worried, I thought I'd got the wrong night" explains Bob

"No, Bob … we'd never let you down, mate" laughs Mike

"Hello, Bob" greets Gez

"Anyway, we're honoured tonight" explains Mike

"Why?" asks Bob

"We've got Mr Leeds with us tonight" advises Mike

"Mr Leeds" laughs David

"I thought I'd better show my face" replies David

Mike and Gez get the beers in …

The Bar starts to fill with lots of Zodiac members … it's a very busy night …

Ernest arrives, and he is his usual witty self …

"Hey, David … fancy seeing you here" laughs Ernest

Next to arrive at Tapas is Sally and Carla …

David motions to Gez and Mike …

"I'll need you both as back up, just in case there's a confrontation" advises David (Looks concerned)

"Yea, very wise, David" replies Mike (pensive)
Sally and Carla go towards
the bar area …
David decides to make his
move …
"Carla" asks David
"That's me, love" replies Carla (Smiles)

"I need to have a word with you" explains David (Looks serious)

"Yea, we need a word in your shell like" quips Mike
"I'm David, the Zodiac Regional Administrator" advises David
"What's this all about?" asks Carla
David motions to Carla to go to the other side of the bar … Carla follows … Mike and Gez are also alongside David …
Lots of Zodiac members are now looking on, and are obviously very intrigued …
"So, what's this all about, David?" asks Carla
"There's no easy way of saying this" explains David
"Why, what have I done?" asks Carla
"I'm afraid your excluded from Zodiac" advises David
"Excluded, why?" asks Carla (Looks

stunned)

"Simply because you broke Zodiac rules … you made fun out of someone by calling them names … now that member won't come again, because of you" explains David (Looks concerned)

"I take it, you know who it is?" asks Mike

"Maybe" laughs Carla

"This is no laughing matter, love" quips Mike

"What about you?" asks Carla (pointing to Gez)

"I thought you liked me?" asks Carla

"You know I do" replies Gez

"Well?" asks Carla

"The truth is … the damage has been done" advises David (Looks serious)

"There are several witnesses" adds David

"So what happens now?" asks Carla

"I'm afraid you'll have to leave immediately" explains David

"Your membership has been cancelled" advises Mike

Carla storms out of Tapas in tears followed by Sally.

Mike, Gez and David return to the bar area …

"What's happened to Rigger Mortice?" quips Ernest (Everyone Laughing)

"I'm afraid she's no longer with us" advises David
"She had a big mouth" adds Ernest

"Well, you may be right on that, Ernest" explains David

"She took the mickey out of loads of people here" explains Ernest

"We know, Ernest" adds Mike
"Sorry gentlemen but it had to be done" advises David
"Don't look so down, Gezza" advises Mike
"I'm OK, but shocked, I suppose" replies Gez

"Rigger Mortice was not right for you lad" advises Ernest
"I was married to a nurse for many years, and I was always rated second fiddle" explains Ernest
"There's plenty of more fish in the sea, mate" advises Mike (Smiling)

"That's right … there's as good a fish in the sea, that ever came out of it, Gezza" advises Ernest (All Laughing)

I'LL GO WHERE THE MUSIC TAKES ME!

Mike and Gez are continuing their conversation at Tapas Bar night …

"There's a party in Harrogate on Saturday … Come as you were when the ship was going down" advises Mike (Laughs)
"That'll be Titanic"
replies Gez (Laughs)
"What do you think,
Gezza?" asks Mike
"You know what, we'll all go, it'll be like a hair of the dog party" explains Mike (Laughing)
"Hair of the dog?" asks Gez (Smiling)

"Oh, you haven't lived till you've been to a hair of the dog party" adds Mike (Laughing)
Ernest enters Tapas and joins Mike and Gez in conversation near the bar …
"I'm just going, as myself" advises Ernest (Smiling)
"Jump … I'll save you" adds Ernest (Laughing)

"What the heck is he on about?" asks
Mike (Laughing)

"You are so rude, Ernest" advises Gez
(Smiling)
"Got to keep up my reputation" insists
Ernest (Laughing)
"It's not your reputation we're worried

about" laughs Mike

Kris arrives at Tapas … Ernest greets her on arrival …

"Did you enjoy Christmas?" asks Ernest (Smiling)

"Oh, it was very enjoyable … such a lovely Christmas day" advises Kris (Winks)

"How was it for you, Gez?" asks Kris
"Oh, pretty spectacular, love" replies Gez (Winks)

Gez pulls Kris to one side …

"More of the same then?" asks Kris (Smiling)
"Absolutely" advises Gez (Laughing)

"Are you on your own tonight, Kris?" asks Gez

"Oh, Stella just wanted me as a taxi service" replies Kris

"I've stopped that … but you can service me anytime" adds Kris (Winking)

"Yes, I will" replies Gez
"Do you fancy coming to the event in Harrogate, Kris?" asks Gez
"When is it, love?" asks Kris (Looks intrigued)
"It's on between now and New Year's Eve" explains Gez
"Oh, I'd love to" replies Kris (Smiling)
Ernest decides to join in the conversation between Kris and Gez …
"You could go in your bathing costume, Kris" advises Ernest (Smiling)
Kris smiles, then

walks away ...
"What did I say?" asks
Ernest
"Was it something I said?" replies Ernest (All Laughing)

Danny and Pat arrive at Tapas and join Mike, Gez and Ernest at the bar ...

"Have we missed anything?" asks Danny
"No ... only Ernest putting his foot in it
again" laughs Mike
"We love you, Ernest ... warts and all"
explains Mike
"Are you both up for the do in
Harrogate?" asks Gez
"Oh, yea ... we're both going to
that" replies Pat
"It sounds a bit fishy"
laughs Danny
"OK, enough of the jokes"
replies Mike
Jack and Sally arrive at Tapas and join everyone in the bar area ...

"Have you got your tickets for the Come as you were Party in Harrogate?" asks Mike (Points to Events Board)
"We've already got out tickets ... are you all going?" asks Jack

"Yea, we've all reserved our tickets too ... it should be a fun night" replies Gez (Smiling)
The night of the Come as you were Party arrives ...

it seems that every Zodiac member has decided to go to the event, which is taking place at the home of Sacha in Harrogate …

Gez, Mike, Ernest, Danny and Pat arrive at the venue with bottles and plate for the party …

"Hi, I'm Sacha" greets a lady at the door (Big Smile)

Sacha is an attractive, elegant, green eyed brunette …

"Hi, I'm Gez … this is Mike, Ernest, Danny and Pat … we're all from Leeds" advises Gez (Smiling)

"Oh, there's more coming from Leeds" explains Sacha

Sacha's home is decked out in all things nautical … which all adds to the occasion!

"We thought we'd have a Limbo contest, later" explains Sacha

"Oh, this is the love boat" laughs Ernest

"Well, how low can you go" quips Mike (Laughing)

"I hope all the ladies are wearing knickers" replies Ernest (All Laughing)

"That'll be a first for you, Ernest" laughs Mike

"Your just an old letch" quips Danny (Laughing)

"Just how old is Ernest?" asks Pat

"Oh, he'll be 60 plus, at least" explains Mike

"There's life in the old dog yet" advises Ernest (Everyone Laughing) "You said it" replies Gez (Laughing)

More and more Zodiac members arrive, and the house is almost at bursting point ...
Mike makes a general comment to all the Zodiac members ...

"Are you all coming to the New Year's Eve Party in Leeds?" asks Mike

"Yes, we've all been invited" advise several members
"OK, just to inform you that it is a SELL OUT" explains Mike (Looks happy)
Gez ponders the New Year's Eve event in Leeds ...
"You know what?"
asks Gez
"What?" asks Mike
"I've never given a New Year's Eve Party before" explains Gez
"Maybe I will, in the future" adds Gez
"We'll all be up for that event, Gezza" replies Mike
"OK, I'll keep you all posted" advises Gez (Smiling)
Kris arrives at the Come as you were party ...
"Well, hello ... Kris" advises Gez (Smiling)
"You look as if your roaring to go" quips Mike (Laughing)
"What have you come as?" asks Ernest (Smiling)

"Oh, I'm a lady from the roaring twenties" replies Kris (Smiling)
" … and yes I'm roaring to go" explains Kris (Laughing)
Gez pulls Kris to one side …
"I bet you are" adds Gez
"Your a bit of a naughty minx" explains Gez (Smiling)
"Oh yea, that's me" adds Kris (Smiling)
"But, only for you, love" explains Kris (Winks)

"By the way, I may have another need later" adds Kris
"Can you help me?" asks Kris (Sexy)

"Oh, don't worry … I'll definitely sort out your need later" explains Gez

Ernest enters the conversation with Kris and Gez …
"Oh, you should always make sure you give them one" adds Ernest (Laughing)
"Very witty … and as quick as a flash too" replies Kris
"Oh, no … I've said flash, he'll pick up on that too" adds Kris (Smiling)
"Well, give me the option" quips Ernest (Laughing)
"Go on give them a flash, they'll love it" adds Ernest (All Laughing)

Mike joins in the banter with Gez, Kris and Ernest …

"Does anyone know what he is going on about?" asks Mike (Laughing)

"Sorry, we haven't got a clue" replies Gez (Laughing)

Meanwhile, the party in Harrogate starts to get into full swing ...

"OK, everyone ... it's Limbo time" announces Sacha

"We need volunteers to do the lowering of the pole?" asks Sacha (Smiling)

"OK, Sacha ... we'll do it, love" replies Mike (Smiling)

"OK, I'll do it too" advises Gez (Smiling)

"Haven't we been here before, Gezza?" asks Mike (Laughing)

"You know we have, Mike" (Laughs)

"OK, ladies ... watch your modesty" advises Mike (Smiling)

"Yea, keep a hand over your modesty too" explains Gez (Smiling)

"Ernest, that's not advice for you" quips Mike (All Laughing)

"You, just be a good boy" replies Gez (Laughing)

"I'm always a good lad, aren't I?" quips Ernest (More Laughing)

Reggae music starts to play in the background ...

"How low can you go?" asks Mike
Ladies and gentlemen line up to take turns in going under the pole …
First up is Kris … and she skilfully manages to go under the pole.
"Up and under" advises Ernest (Smiling)
"How did I do?" asks Kris (Smiling)

"I didn't show my knickers,
did I?" asks Kris (Looks
embarrassed)

"No, not at all, Kris" advises
Gez (Smiling)
"That's OK then … but I will for you later" replies Kris (Winking)
"Hey, keep the pole steady, Gezza" advises Mike (Laughing)
"Oh, I will, Mike" replies Gez (Laughing)
A few more ladies manage to get under the pole successfully …
"You've all done it, before" advises Mike (Smiling)
"Hey, I saw your knickers, then" advises Ernest (Laughing)
"Glad you enjoyed the show" replies a blonde lady (Smiling)
"You can get it if you really want it" adds the blonde lady
"No comment from you, Ernest" replies Mike (Laughing)
It was another great night, and it put everyone in

the mood for the New Year's Eve party a few days later …

The evening of the New Year's Eve party arrives …

Everyone is beginning to congregate for the party of the year at Terri's house.

Gez is in fancy dress and goes as
a Spaceman …

"Hi, I'm Gez" greets Terri (Big
Kiss)
"Welcome to my home … yes I know who you are Gez, have we met before?" asks Terri (Smiling)
Terri is a stunning blonde, blue eyes, and wearing a skimpy outfit …
"Maybe at Tapas?" asks Gez (Smiling)
"No, I think I've seen you before, somewhere" adds Terri
"Can't think where, Terri" replies Gez (Looks concerned)

"Maybe in town or somewhere
recent" explains Terri

"Your beginning to freak me out"
laughs Gez
"OK, refreshments and drinks, over there, please" advises Terri (points to kitchen)
"Oh, I'm driving so it'll have to be softly, softly for me" advises Gez (Smiling)
"I hope that's not everything" laughs Terri
"Cheeky … now that would be telling"
replies Gez (Laughing)
"Flattery will get you everywhere"

explains Terri (Big Smile)
"I like your tight outfit" replies Gez
"Oh, I'm glad you like it, love … I'm supposed to be Cat woman" replies Terri (Smiling)
"And a nice little pussy, at that" advises Gez (Laughing)
"Cheeky" replies Terri (Laughing)
"Has anyone arrived from Leeds yet?" asks Gez

"Yes, mostly are in fancy dress and in disguise … see if you can recognise any of them?" explains Terri
Gez begins to mingle, and dodges away from more questioning from Terri … Someone has turned up as the Mad Hatter, and to be honest, Gez has no idea who they are …
"It's me" says a
voice "Who?" asks
Gez (Laughing)
"Ernest … see I fooled you" quips Ernest (Laughing)
"What do you think of the gear?"
asks Ernest (Looks great)
"It took me hours to put on" explains Ernest (Laughing)
"Ernest, you took me by surprise"
replies Gez (Laughing)
"I'd never have guessed it was you"
explains Gez
More and more Zodiac members arrive at the New Year's Eve party … Danny arrives as a very green hulk …

"Danny is that you?" asks Ernest
(Looks shocked)
"Yes, it's me, Ernest" replies
Danny (Laughing)
"I thought I'd give this a whirl again, mate" explains Danny

"Oh, the ladies will go mad for you tonight" advises Ernest (Laughing)

"Look at you, though" replies Danny
"You've really pushed the boat out, Ernest" adds Danny (Laughing)
"They'll all go for you tonight, too, Ernest" replies Danny
Gez moves across the floor to greet Danny …
"Don't tell me, your from outer space?" asks Danny
"Flesh Gordon, isn't it?" asks Ernest (Laughing)
"How did you guess, Ernest?" laughs Gez
"What about me?" asks Ernest

"Ernest, with your reputation at Zodiac … any woman is on your radar" quips Gez (Laughing)
"We'll have some fun tonight" replies Ernest (Smiling)
Mike arrives at the New Year's Eve party in fancy dress …
"Great costume, Mike" advises Gez (Laughing)

Mike has come as Bertie Basset …

"You'll get eaten alive, tonight, Mike" adds Gez (All Laughing)

"Very funny … it's hot in here mate" explains Mike
"I don't think it's so hot yet" replies Ernest (Smiles)
"No, not in the room … in this suit" adds Mike (Laughing)

"Come on Bertie … you need something to cool you down" advises Gez (All Laughing)

Mike, Ernest, Danny and Gez head for the beer tent, which is an extension from the French windows into an outdoor tent area …
"Right, where's my booze?" asks Mike
"What are you having, Mike?" asks Gez (Points to Beer tent)
"A can of lager, mate … what about you?" replies Mike
"Oh, I'm driving … so something soft" advises Gez
"A word to the wise, Gezza … don't tell all the girls here that your going soft" explains Mike (Everyone Laughing)
Next to arrive at the New Year's Eve party is Kris … dressed as a belly dancer …
"Don't you recognise me?" asks Kris (Looks stunning)
"No, not really" advises Gez

(Looks puzzled)
"It's me, Kris" replies Kris (Big Smile)
"Oh, wow, I didn't recognise you in that" explains Gez

"I'll do a special belly dance for your later, love" replies Kris (Winks)

"I'll do my dance of the seven veils" explains Kris
"What's that?" asks Gez (Looks puzzled)

"Oh, I'll only be dressed in seven veils, and I'll dance for you, then at the end …" adds Kris (Smiling)
"Oh, I get the picture, Kris" laughs Gez
"Well, what do you think?" asks Kris
"I think I'm going to love it, Kris" replies Gez
"I thought you might" quips Kris (Smiling)
The party starts to get into full swing and everyone is in the mood for dancing …
Jack and Sally arrive at the New Year's Eve party, and are, as always inseparable!
"You know what?" asks Ernest
"No, what, mate?" replies Mike

"I really don't know why they bother to come now, do you?" asks Ernest

"Who?" asks Mike (Looks around)

"Jack and Sally" adds Ernest

"Well, for once, your right, Ernest … neither do I" replies Mike (Laughs)

"I've got absolutely no idea either" replies Gez

Kris comes over to Mike, Gez and Ernest … and whispers into Gez's ear …

"Do you want rescuing, love?" asks Kris (Smiling)

"Oh, yea … just in the nick of time" replies Gez (Smiling)

"The Spaceman and the Belly Dancer … what a combination" quips Mike (All Laughing)

"Where's Danny, the green man got to?" asks Ernest (Laughing)

"Oh, Danny's entertaining a couple of newbies, last time I saw him" replies Gez

"Jack the lad" quips Mike (All Laughing)
"A bit like you then"
replies Gez
"You know what?"
asks Mike
"I'm going to join him" replies
Mike (Laughing)
"Are you coming, Ernest?" asks
Mike
"Try and stop me" laughs Ernest

Kris and Gez start to get close
to each other …

"Put your hand on my bum" asks Kris (Smiling)

"Don't mind if I do" quips Gez
"That's it ... hold on to your Belly dancer's back side" explains Kris (Winks)
"Kris, you are so naughty" replies Gez (Laughing)
"You like it, don't you?" asks Kris (Smiling)
"Oh, yea, of course I do" replies Gez (Smiling)

More Zodiac members arrive at the New Year's Eve party ...

Jane and Lucy from York look very attractive in their short nurses outfits ...

"Ernest, no looking for kind nurses, tonight, OK?" asks Mike (Laughing)

"Oh, spoilsport ... OK, I promise ... no heavy petting" laughs Ernest

Danny and Mike look concerned ...
"Has he had one or two or what?" asks Mike (Looks puzzled)
"Who knows, perhaps he has" replies Danny
"OK, we'd better keep and eye on him" explains Mike
"Where's Gez?" asks Danny
"He's looking after Kris, tonight ... lucky man" replies Mike (Winks)

Pat arrives at the New Year's Eve party dressed as a gangster …

"OK, you dirty rats … this is a hold up" advises Pat (Laughing)

"Dirty rats, indeed" replies Mike (Laughing)
"Look at you two" replies Pat (Laughing)

"Well, we thought we'd make the effort" explains Mike (Laughing)

"Just, like me" adds Pat (Laughs)
Jane and Lucy come over to talk to Mike, Ernest and Pat …

"You'd better not bend over in that … we'll see what you had for breakfast, if you do, love" quips Ernest (Laughing)
"We'll be careful" replies
Jane (Smiling)
"Is he OK?" asks Mike
(Looks concerned)
"I think he's had one over the eight, Mike" replies Pat

"I'm OK, lad" adds Ernest

Terri makes an announcement to all Zodiac members …

"OK, everyone … bubbly and a present for everyone at Midnight" advises Terri

The special evening continues, and more and more Zodiac members arrive … this is an exclusive event … members only!
Meanwhile, Danny and Gez decide it's time for a refill in the beer tent … Someone is taking photos in there to mark the New Year's Eve event …
"Come on in, you two" advises Bob
"Would you like your photos taken with Little Bo Peep and Robin Hood (female version)?" asks Bob
"Yea, why not … are you up for it Gezza?"
asks Danny (Smiling)
"OK, I agree … lets do it" replies Gez (Smiling)
"OK, girls … sit on their
laps" orders Bob
Both girls get on their laps
as instructed …
"When I shout snog em go for it"
quips Bob (Laughing)
"OK … one … two … three … snog
em" advises Bob
"Perfect photo" advises Bob
"It's freezing in this beer tent" advise the girls

"Well, it is the 31st of December" replies Gez (Laughing)

"I'm really enjoying myself tonight" advises Danny (Laughing)

"I've brought a tape or two with me, to liven things up later" quips Danny

"Perfect" replies Gez
"We'll do a lot of events next year" advises Gez
"What have you got in mind?" asks Danny
"Well, are you up for it?" asks Gez
"OK, count me in" replies Danny

"We'll do the ITV TELETHON 92 …what do you think, Danny?" asks Gez (Looks excited)

"Oh, yes I'm in for all of that … and I can't wait to get started" responds Danny

"Oh, it'll be lots of fun … and exposure for Zodiac" advises Gez
"Robert has already planned for a Live Event in the Main Arena at Harewood House on Telethon day" explains Gez
"What do Yorkshire Television say?" asks Danny
"They think it's fantastic and are in on it" replies Gez
"It sounds amazing" advises Danny
"I don't really know what Robert has got up his sleeve" explains Gez

"His arm" laughs Danny
"Oh, very witty, Danny" adds Gez (Laughing)

Robert arrives at the New Year's Eve party dressed as Sweeney Todd with Beth, she is all dolled up …
"We were wondering where you had got to Rob?" greets Gez
"Oh, we thought we would delay our arrival" replies Rob
"There are lots of ladies here tonight" advises Rob (Smiling)
"Oh, yea … Danny is overwhelmed" explains Gez (Laughing)
Lucy joins Gez and Robert …
"Where's our green man?" asks Lucy
"Oh, I'm here love" replies Danny (Smiling)

"OK, fellas, I'll see you later … duty calls" explains Danny (Laughing)

The music changes to 80s pop …

"Oh, they are playing my song" shouts Ernest (All Laughing)

"It's just for you, Ernest" quips Mike
Kris comes over to Gez and asks him directly …

"Hey, when are you dancing with me, love?" asks Kris (Smiling)

"Now, darling" replies Gez (Big Smile)
It's just before Midnight … Danny takes a tape out of his pocket … Everyone is on the dance floor …

Suddenly the bongs of Big Ben ring out the old and ring in the new …
"Happy New Year" shouts Terri (All Laugh)
"Happy 1992" shouts Mike (All Cheering)

Terri is surrounded by various male members.

After lots of kissing and smooching it's back to the party …

"OK, it's present time" advises Terri
Every member of Zodiac puts their hand in a black bag and pulls out something to remind them of the New Year's Eve party …
Its quite unbelievable … it's a mini vibrator for all the ladies and various gifts for the men!
It was all taken in good fun, and part of the atmosphere of the occasion.
"What am I going to do with this" asks Ernest (Laughing)
Ernest is on the receiving end of a plastic mini vibrator!
"Well, I know what I'm going to do with mine" explains Kris
"Now you've got two willies,Ernest … me old cock sparrow" advises Mike (Everyone Laughing)
"Yea, but what can I do with it?" asks Ernest (All Laughing)

"Well, you can use it to water your plants, if you turn it upside down" laughs Mike (All Laughing)
"Well, I never" laughs Ernest
 "I've never seen you lost for words, Ernest" advises Gez (Smiling)

"OK, everyone ... it's time for SIMPLY THE BEST" advises Terri
Everyone piles on to the dance floor ...
It's wasn't the end but the dawn of a new era and the voyage of discovery all over again ...
But where's Gez?

Why did he suddenly leave the New Year's Eve party without telling anyone?

Who is he, and why is he still hiding a secret?
All will be revealed in the follow up ...

IT'S STILL A KIND OF LOVE

COPYRIGHT@2024
GERRY CULLEN

IT'S STILL A KIND OF LOVE

It's back to 1992 in this follow up to It's A Kind of Love.

This comedy/drama is based on a true and original story, set at Zodiac Singles Club in Leeds, heralding a new era!
Gez returns with Mike and Co to help raise funds with a series of events for the ITV TELETHON 92.
It all comes together in an "on the day" event in the Main Arena at Harewood House with a Truck Pull challenge against the Emmerdale Team … and a giant cheque presentation to Yorkshire Television!
The drama is set in Leeds. It showcases Yorkshire comedy at its best with everyday normal routines … but things are never normal at Zodiac!

When Gez returns to Zodiac after a mysterious disappearance, questions are obviously being asked. Mike and Ernest are on hand to make a success of everything Gez does. But … Gez is still hiding a secret …
Who is he? Why does he appear mysterious?
Heart warming characters and dialogue make this story stand out. All will be revealed in the coming stories …
It's Still A Kind of Love shows people at their very best, in all sorts of comical, true to life, situations!

BETWEEN WORLDS: MY TRUE COMA STORY

Gerry Cullen

GERRY CULLEN has written a unique and mesmerising book.

Gerry's true-life story includes an account of when he woke up after having major open-heart surgery in a Leeds hospital in March 2018. He received an unexpected gift from his induced coma.

Where had this gift of writing come from? Why had he received it?

On reflection, Gerry now feels that he is incredibly lucky to have received this Heaven-Sent gift. This life changing event and its aftermath have become a blessing in his life.

Gerry began to write profusely since that time; an astonishing development, as he had never authored any books or scripts before the coma.

Four years prior to his heart surgery, Gerry

experienced a spiritual awakening, and regular messages were coming to him in his dreams. They were a major source of comfort to him.

Gerry believes that people in comas are living 'between worlds' and that their friends and family members are also living between worlds with them.

The messages from above have continued ever since and today his writing is flourishing. He has a fascinating tale to tell; it is a story of our times with many lessons for those with eyes to see and ears to hear!

The plot is a true-life account based around a fascinating subject of otherworldly connections.

Gerry's life story is full of encounters with another realm, the spiritual one. The pacing is good throughout. The book is well thought out as each chapter flows logically.

Author's Voice - The author's voice broadly means the written style of the book, covering tone, syntax, and grammar, amongst other things. It can be thought of as how the book is written.

Gerry is a good writer; I liked his style and voice. I was interested as the book progressed to discover more and it intrigued me.

This book could be a powerful memoir of Gerry's life and times, and the Heaven-Sent gift of writing that he received after open heart surgery. I liked reading about his visions and encounters with the spirit world and the supernatural realm of life; it's quite fascinating. I liked the examination of current events and times at the end of the book. too.

All in all, a great read for any person interested in life beyond our earth plane.

Many books have been adapted to film from this genre, for example, 90 Minutes in Heaven, an extremely popular movie, with over 1,800 reviews on Amazon Prime.

I feel that Gerry's book would make a great movie too.

It's a heart-warming and touching story of a man's journey and how he goes through a life changing operation that leaves him with a wonderful gift.

I loved the insights beyond our normal senses' range into another realm that will guide us if only we would allow it to do so. In these times that we find ourselves in, I feel Gerry's testimony in the book, and his many anecdotes and stories, will demonstrate that there are more dimensions to behold than what we know in a three-dimensional world.

Report provided by Janet Lee Chapman, in September 2021, on behalf of Susan Mears Film and Literary Agency and Merlin Agency

ABOUT THE AUTHOR

Gerry Cullen

GERRY CULLEN My first book, BETWEEN WORLDS: MY TRUE COMA STORY, is a true adaptation of what happened to me, before and after, having major open heart surgery at Leeds General Infirmary in March 2018.

It is a very real and true account of the "gift" I received after being in an induced coma.

My second book, SKY HIGH! COTE D'AZUR, and my third book ANGEL'S EYES/CHRISTMAS ANGELS are both adapted from my series of stories, written for television.

I had never written books or for television prior to being in a coma.

My very real and true story continues today!

FOLLOW MY STORY ON TWITTER -

@GerryCullen15

PRAISE FOR AUTHOR

Reviewed in the United Kingdom on 16 May 2022
An excellent book showing that there is far more to life then we realise and that there is a continuation of our soul after the death of our body.

Reviewed in the United Kingdom on 21 April 2022
Verified Purchase
With truly moving frankness the author narrates a life-threatening experience and how it brought him closer to his spiritual life.

Reviewed in the United Kingdom on 20 May 2022
A great read and one that really makes you think

Reviewed in the United Kingdom on 12 August 2022
This book was of particular interest to me because of my line of work. I love hearing about people's experiences with things that are on a different vibration to us earthly beings. The spiritual awakenings that people go through have been documented and discussed since the beginning of time and each person's story is unique in

its own way, there are always some similarities on the surface but I encourage you to look a little deeper - you can start with this book…….

The author begins by telling us a little about himself and his life growing up. He then goes into detail about the 'messages' he has received in dreams, these are set out in a sort of diary entry format. He also speaks of visions.

All of the incidents described seem quite insignificant on their own, but when you put them all together they give a much bigger and clearer picture.

There is a lot I could say about this book but seriously, we would be here all day! It's a great read that is sure to inspire and provoke discussion. It really doesn't matter what walk of life you are from, whether you are religious or a non believer. I feel the story should be taken for what it is and that is one gentleman's extraordinary, unique and beautiful experiences which he has chosen to share with the world.

The book, its content and the author himself are a true gift to the world.

5 stars

⭐⭐⭐⭐⭐

- BETWEEN WORLDS: MY TRUE COMA STORY

A 3 star rating on Amazon to date with no comments

- SKY HIGH: COTE D'AZUR

Reviewed in the United Kingdom on 13 December 2023 "Angels Eyes" by Gerry Cullen is a heartwarming and enchanting collection of seasonal stories that follows the adventures of Rebecca, Mary, John Paul, and Nicola, who have been reassigned by Michael the Archangel to become proprietors of the CHRISTMAS ANGELS shop in York. As they assume their roles as shopkeepers with a difference, the Angels become involved in a series of angelic and human situations that are filled with the magic of Christmas.

Set in various locations in York, the stories are imbued with a magical Christmas feeling that is sure to warm the hearts of readers. The characters' true identities as Angels are kept secret throughout the stories, adding an element of mystery and intrigue.

"Angels Eyes" is a delightful and uplifting read that captures the spirit of Christmas and the joy of the holiday season. Gerry Cullen's writing is engaging and filled with charm, making this book a perfect choice for anyone looking for a heartwarming holiday read.

- ANGEL'S EYES: CHRISTMAS ANGELS

No comments have yet been left for this book.

- THE VATICAN MONSIGNOR - THE SAVIOUR'S COMING

BOOKS BY THIS AUTHOR

Between Worlds: My True Coma Story

This true-life story includes an account of what happened to Gerry Cullen before and after waking up, having had major open-heart surgery at Leeds General Infirmary in March 2018, and the "gift" received from being in an induced coma.
Gerry explains his new found gift within the book. But where it had come from and why he received it, remains a mystery to this day.

A spiritual awakening with messages received in dreams and other unworldly encounters, makes this story a fascinating read, leaving us wondering about life itself and beyond.

Sky High: Cote D'azur

Nice, sun kissed jewel of the French Riviera. A popular tourist destination for the rich and famous.

When a British MI6 agent goes missing after being on attachment to the Commissariat de Police in Nice, a Specialist Task Force is set up on the Cote D'Azur to assist the Police in cracking crime on the Continent.

Three "Ghost Operatives" are drafted in by British Intelligence under an alias. Countess Suzanna Minori is placed in charge of unit in liaison with Mark Taylor in London.

In a series of assignments on the Cote D'Azur and in London suave Simon King, rough diamond Steve McBride and new recruit Bethany Williams are the "ghost" agents working under the code name: SKY HIGH!

Amazing picturesque locations on the French Riviera taking in Monte Carlo, Monaco, Cannes and Nice add to the charm, character and atmosphere of the series of stories.

Stylish, chic, gripping with just the right amount of panache!

Action adventure guaranteed!

C'est la vie!

Angel's Eyes: Christmas Angels

ANGEL'S EYES - The Angel private eyes, with a difference, undertake anything with a twist, they are all real angels!

Angel's: Rebecca, Mary, John Paul and Nicola have been sent by Michael the Archangel to LEEDS, West Yorkshire, and the ancient city of YORK to investigate all types of problems, from all levels of society.

The Angel's are aiming to find, and guide, lost souls, to protect those in distress, and to help those without a cause.

They have been charged to give sight to those who cannot see, whatever the problem, and to heal the sick and incurable.

All the Angel's will have to undertake their assignments while also being human on Earth at the same time!

They do not want to get their wings, they already have them!

While under the protection of Heaven, they will also be able to cloak themselves in disguise!

The Angel's are ready to assist anyone who needs their help in this stylish set of stories.

The Angel's will encounter the Grey Lady, the ghostly Centurion and a cohort of Roman soldiers, Dick Turpin and Guy Fawkes along the way.

The Angel's will also experience Speed Dating and various other problems in a very modern day World!

CHRISTMAS ANGELS - This seasonal set of stories reunites Rebecca, Mary, John Paul and Nicola.

The Angel's have been reassigned by Michael the Archangel and assume the roles of Proprietors of the famous CHRISTMAS ANGELS shop in YORK, on a short term lease, with a view to being permanent!
However, they are shop keepers with a difference!
The Angel's become engaged in various angelic and human situations, all with a magical Christmas feeling!
The stories take place at various settings in YORK.
Will the Angel's be found out, or will their true identities remain an angelic secret?

The Vatican Monsignor - The Saviour's Coming

THE VATICAN MONSIGNOR

Monsignor Kevin O'Flaherty is no ordinary priest. He loves the classics, has a taste for golf and Guinness, all things Irish, and a nose for solving the unknown. The Monsignor is Head of Investigations at the Vatican. He reports directly to Cardinal Raphael and His Holiness, the Pope … Supreme Pontiff of Rome.
In this series of stories, The Monsignor, investigates into various mystical phenomena, around the World. The Saviour's Coming is based on the Blessed Trinity … God in three persons, and it's the Monsignor's first investigation.
The Monsignor is assigned by Cardinal Raphael and the Holy Father. He teams up with Professor "Max"

Brookstein in New York after being summoned by the Cardinal to investigate into recent, ongoing, unknown, unexplained phenomenon.

World governments are in a panic when earthquakes, famines and great signs appear in the sky …

When an earthquake takes place in New York city, followed by the threat of a huge tidal wave, the Monsignor and "Max" devise a plan … but will it work, and just how long do they have before it's too late? Is The Second Coming about to happen … and does it signal the end of the World … as we know it?

The Monsignor also investigates into … The Ten Plagues of Egypt … a phenomenon surrounding Mary Magdalen, the Arc of the Covenant and the Book of Galileo.

A gripping series of pulsating psychological, intrigue and mystery, with heart pounding twists and turns every step of the way! With a breath taking setting in Rome and around the World.

The adventure is just beginning!

Printed in Great Britain
by Amazon